ELLA'S ENIGMA

ANNA AYSGARTH

Ella's Enigma

ISBN: 979-8-88653-455-9

Published by Satin Romance
An Imprint of Melange Books, LLC
White Bear Lake, MN 55110
www.satinromance.com

Published in the United States of America.

Cover Design by Ashley Redbird Designs

To my sister, Elaine, we have laughed together, cried together and sometimes moaned together, but always faced the world together.

PROLOGUE

Lady Ella Grainger turned her horse, Beauty, back towards Swallowfield. It would soon be getting dark, days in December were short and there was a hint of snow in the air. From her position on top of the hill at the edge of the estate she sighed as she saw the carriage travelling up the long, tree lined drive. She did not need to see the crest on the side to know it belonged to Stephen Thorne, Duke of Hart.

Her sister, Verity, had broken the news only this morning that he would be joining them for Christmas. For Verity's sake she had appeared happy at the news, but had she known, she would have gone with her younger sister Caro, to visit her friend or she would have gladly accompanied her aged Aunt Bette to France. Anything would have been better than facing Stephen, the man who had proposed to her, not from love, or even for the generous dowry her brother-in-law had provided for he had no need of it. No, he had offered to marry her out of pity and because he needed an heir, but mostly because he thought she was desperate, and frankly it was just convenient to him.

It was clear he thought that she would fall at his feet with gratitude because he believed that, like her father, no other man would ever make an offer. She had been told all her life that she was ugly and cursed and no man would ever want to bed her unless the candles were out and the curtains drawn and they certainly would not want to look at her in the light. Her father had blamed her for everything that had gone wrong in his life, the loss of his fortune as well as his failure to sire a male heir. It was all her fault, his cursed child.

Her hand unconsciously went to the almost invisible scar down the side of her face where she had been burnt as a babe. Her father, the late earl almost seemed to take pleasure in taunting her, his words were etched on her brain: she was disfigured, she was a freak, a monster. On more than one occasion he had told her it would have been better if she had died in the fire. There was no coming out ball for her, why should he waste the money for no man would want her. While her father was alive, she had been almost hidden away, kept out of sight so that the sight of her would not offend anyone. It was only the love and acceptance of her step-mothers and step-sisters that she had gained some self-respect, but her father's words were imprinted on her brain. 'You are a monster, no-one will want you, no-one will love you, you are unlovable.' The physical scars had faded, in a way the mental scars never would.

After giving her horse to a groom, Ella entered the house by a side rather than the grand front entrance in the hope of putting off meeting the duke a little longer.

"Ah, there you are," her sister's voice rang out. "What are you doing, skulking about? Stephen has arrived."

"I noticed," Ella replied.

"And that is no doubt why you are skulking." Verity raised an elegant eyebrow.

"I was not skulking, I was merely ensuring that I did not traipse mud all over the floor," she lied.

Verity said nothing but looked down at her immaculate riding boots. "Well, Stephen is here and I have just ordered tea, so please come and join us in the blue drawing room."

"I thought I might change first..." Ella began.

The duchess took a deep breath. "I know this might feel a little awkward, not having seen Stephen for such a long time, especially given the fact that you did not part on the best of terms, but please, for the sake of the children at least, try to make his visit here a pleasant one. It is not often he is able to spend it with his family at Christmastide, and we are his family."

"Very well," Ella said with a sigh. "I just wish you had told me he was coming."

"I did tell you, and I thought you and Caro were excited to see him again."

Ella shook her head. "Caro was excited since she does not know the full story and I just pinned a smile on my face and pretended for her sake and yours. I did not want to spoil the celebrations, especially for the children, but to be honest I do not know how I feel about seeing him again, perhaps I should not have come after all."

"That would never do, you are my sister, and I want you here, but more than that, I want you to enjoy yourself," Verity replied with a hopeful smile. "Besides, it is time you two put the past behind you. Now come along, the tea will be getting cold."

Stephen Thorne, Duke of Hart warmed his hands by the blazing fire. It had been six years since he had spent time with his brother, other than a few fleeting visits. His work, officially as a diplomat, had meant that he had spent the last few years abroad in the service of king and country, but in truth he had been only too happy to leave the country so that he would not come across Lady Ella Grainger. The fact that she had roundly rejected him still rankled, the fact that she was his sister-in-law made matters extremely complicated.

"Here." His brother held out a glass. "This should warm the cockles better than the tea my dear wife will foist on you shortly."

Stephen laughed. "I am looking forward to seeing Verity again, meeting my nephew and seeing my nieces, though it is so long since I have seen them that I doubt they will remember me."

Elliott took a breath. "There is someone else here you will perhaps be less keen to meet," he said, hesitant. "Ella is spending Christmas with us. Her Aunt Bette with whom she spends much of her time, has gone to the south of France for her health."

Stephen's glass paused halfway to his mouth, before he downed the amber liquid in one gulp. "Why did you not tell me before?" he demanded.

"Because I knew you would not come," Elliott replied with a grin. "Verity is of the opinion, as am I, that it is high time you two settled your differences. Christmastide is, after all, a time for peace and goodwill."

"Let us hope so, brother, let us hope so." Stephen held out his glass. "I hope you have a goodly supply of this. I have a feeling I am going to need it."

CHAPTER 1

Ella surveyed herself in the cheval mirror. Verity had relented and allowed her ten minutes to change out of her riding clothes and into a suitable day dress. As she was no longer a very young woman, she did not feel the need to wear the pastel colours debutantes were obliged to wear, she chose what colours she liked, and the rich red velvet perfectly complimented her creamy skin and set off the auburn highlights in her dark hair. As always it was fastened in a chignon with loose curls teased out to hide the faint scars on the side of her face. She stuck her tongue out at her reflection. It will have to do; if Stephen Alexander Thorne does not like it, he will have to lump it. Straightening her shoulders she marched down to the blue drawing room.

As she entered, the two men stood up and bowed as she curtseyed. In spite of herself, her eyes were drawn instantly to the Duke of Hart. He was just as tall and imposing as he had been when she had last seen him, several years ago. His dark hair still fell over his forehead though there were a few silver strands at the sides. He had obviously spent time in the sun as his tanned skin emphasised the deep blue of his eyes which were watching her with a degree of curiosity.

"Lady Ella, an unexpected pleasure." His voice was like rich, dark chocolate.

"For me also, Your Grace," she replied.

There was a palpable release of tension in the room, the first few words would surely be the most difficult.

"Come and sit down," Verity said as she poured the tea. "I am sorry, but Caro will not be joining up this evening, much as she was looking forward to seeing you again, Stephen. Before we knew for certain that you were able to come, she had arranged to see Lady Alison Cowper, with whom she was at school. Lady Alison has just married and moved only a few miles away. Naturally, Caro could not resist visiting, but of course, she will return for the festivities."

Stephen watched through hooded eyes as Ella walked gracefully across the room. The young woman he remembered had become an elegant and poised woman, her youthful prettiness had matured into beauty, though he knew she would never believe it because of the damned scars, both the visible and invisible ones. In point of fact, he could see that the physical scars had faded to be almost negligible, the only person who did not see that, he suspected, was Ella. Were her late, unlamented father still alive, Stephen would have happily killed him, for he knew the old earl had much to answer for in respect of his treatment of all his daughters. He took a sip of tea, his sister-in-law had, as predicted pressed on him, his ears attuned to Ella's low, husky voice as she asked her sister about the plans for the coming days. He had always found her voice arousing and was dismayed to find that it still did.

"Now, Elliott and I need to go up to the nursery. Elliott is much in demand as the reader of stories," Verity said, rising from her seat. "So we will leave you two to get reacquainted," she said with a smile. Then added with a raised eyebrow, "I doubt you need a chaperone now. Dinner will be at eight."

Ella watched with alarm as her sister and brother-in-law linked arms and strolled out of the room.

"You do not need to look so fearful, Lady Ella, I am not about to take a bite out of you." The amused voice sounded rather closer than she had realised.

"I am not fearful in the slightest," she replied. "It would take more than you, Duke, to frighten me," she added for good measure.

He laughed. Ella had always been able to make him laugh. "Words I would do well to remember."

"You never married?" he could not help asking, inwardly wincing at his abrupt change of topic and wondering why it was important that he knew.

Ella rolled her eyes. "No. Proposals have been rather thin on the ground. As I once told my sister, why would a man want a flawed woman when he could have a flawless one."

"If you are referring to..." he began.

"The scars are all anyone sees. I have had many years experiencing looks ranging from curiosity to downright revulsion," she interrupted.

"I was not going to refer to them," he replied, quietly. He had barely noticed them. It was a travesty, if anyone should be happily married and raising a family, it was the woman in front of him, the woman he had wanted for his own wife, the woman who had made it patently clear that she did not want him. There was a long pause while he dredged his mind for a suitable topic of conversation.

So what have you done in the time since I last saw you?" he asked, feeling the need to fill the silence.

She rolled her eyes again. "What do you think? I spend a lot of time with my aunt who is not in good health, so the usual female pursuits of embroidering endless cushions which no-one wants to sit on, painting watercolours that no-one wants to look at, and playing the pianoforte, which no-one with functioning ears would want to listen to and which, by the way, I loathe, but Aunt Bette still believes that single young women must be decorative and accomplished rather than educated and informed. I also take tea with the few old ladies who still come to call, read and walk or ride in the park. Not exactly the mad social whirl," she finished, not having intended to reveal so much.

"I thought you were living here with your sister."

"I spend some time here of course, but I do not want to impose myself on Elliott and Verity too much, they have their own family now and Aunt Bette is growing older and needs me. She was very kind to us and, despite her rather old-fashioned notions, it is my pleasure to help assist her now."

"Then why did you not travel to France with your aunt for Christmas?"

She smiled. "She insisted I accept the invitation to spend Christmas at Swallowfield, saying I would have far more fun here with Verity and the children than with an old lady. Though," she added with a small sigh, "the thought of travel was exciting."

"You wish to travel?"

She smiled a sad smile. "I doubt you would understand, given the fact that there are few if any restrictions placed on your life, but the life of a woman is made small by the continual restrictions placed on her. Who she may meet, where she may go and with whom. How she must behave, what topics of conversation she may engage in, how she must laugh, and God forbid that she be caught talking to a man on her own, that is social suicide. And any woman who shows the slightest intelligence is taught from an early age to hide it, because apparently an intelligent woman is a fearsome thing, and an educated one is quite frankly seen as a monster. Our sole purpose in life it seems, is to be decorative and to bear children, preferably males. We are permanently kept in a state of childhood dependence as though we are puppets or dolls to be brought out and admired for our prettiness and put away when we have been played with, and in my case, I didn't even have that."

He hid a smile. God she was magnificent when she was angry. "It is the way society has been ordered for hundreds of years. A man provides for his family, and a woman tends the home." He knew he was prodding at her temper, but he could not seem to help himself. She was already the interesting young woman he remembered rather than the downcast maiden he might have been expecting.

"Then it should change," she replied. "Women should be educated to the same level as men and able to achieve their potential as men are encouraged to do."

"It would seem that you have been reading the works of Mrs. Wollstonecraft."

"Every woman should," she shot back, "and would if they could all read. Rather Mrs. Wollstonecraft's point I think."

He steepled his fingers. "So what you are saying is that females should be educated to the same degree as men?"

"I do. Especially in mathematics and science, there are those who believe that female brains cannot cope with such things, indeed there are some who believe that females using their brains will lead them to become unable to bear children, which is, to my mind, ridiculous."

"I rather tend to agree with you," he replied, surprising her. "And if you were granted this newfound freedom, what would you do with it?"

"I should have liked to study at university, and I would like to travel to the countries I have read about in books, alone if necessary or with a like-minded friend. I do not want to be the poor maiden aunt all my life, just once I want adventure before I settle down to my life of spinsterhood," she finished with a wry smile.

"I am sure that neither Elliott nor Verity think of you as a poor maiden aunt," he replied.

Her eyes shot to his. "Of course not, they have been more than kind and generous, but even the dowry Elliott funded was not enough to tempt a suitor."

"You did have a suitor, and you turned him down," he pointed out.

She took a breath and turned her head so that he could not see the pain in her eyes which she knew would give her away. Yes, she wanted adventure, to travel and have a degree of independence, but she would have loved to have had a home and family of her own. "I could not marry someone for the wrong reasons, I saw enough of that with my father," she said quietly. "Now , if you will excuse me, I should like to see the children before I have to dress for dinner." She was out of the room almost before Stephen stood up.

He sat down and stared into the flames. His brother was right, had he known that Ella would be here, he would never have come. Even now, after all these years he still felt the same pain of rejection. Some men were made to love many women, he was not, there was only one woman he had ever loved, one woman he would only ever love and that woman could not, it seemed, accept it or even see it. He went over to the table and poured himself another brandy, his thoughts turned back to the day he had proposed to Ella, it had been here, at Swallowfield, in the garden, shortly after Verity's kidnap and rescue by Elliott. He realised, after consideration, he had made a complete hash of it. 'I think we should marry, Ella, neither of us is getting younger, I need an heir, and you need a home. I doubt you will get other offers. As to the scars, think nothing of them, they do not matter to me in the slightest.'

"Fool," he muttered, downing the brandy. Had he been in his own home he would have dashed the glass into the fire. "What a complete, bloody fool, no wonder she turned you down, you idiot. You made it sound as though you were doing her a huge favour and marrying her either out of pity or necessity, you pompous ass."

"Well, I didn't hear the beginning of the sentence brother," Elliott laughed as he entered the room, "but I have to say I completely agree with the bit about the pompous ass."

"Brotherly love as always," Stephen replied.

"Forgive me if I am barking up the wrong tree, but would your sentiments have anything to do with your meeting with Ella?" Elliott asked, coming further into the room.

"Bullseye," Stephen replied.

"I know you were fond of her."

"I was...am," Stephen admitted.

"Then you must woo her, now, while you are here without distractions. You may not have another chance."

"Easier said than done, Brother. I rather think I had my chance and I ruined it," Stephen replied.

"I recall you giving me some rather good advice when my own marriage did not get off to the best start, so now I shall return the favour. It seems to me that there are two choices before you," Elliott began, "either you give in and the woman you want is lost to you or you fight for her. The question is, which will you choose?"

"Would that it were that simple. My life is...somewhat complicated," Stephen replied, cryptically.

CHAPTER 2

"So, tell me about this complication," Elliott said as soon as Verity and Ella left the two men to their port. "I know you work for the government, but I begin to suspect, given the amount of time you spend on the continent, that you are not counting beans or sacks of hay in order to levy some ridiculous tax."

Stephen smiled. "You know very well what I do, brother."

Elliott grinned back. "Of course, one does not engage in trade without knowing something of how our government works abroad. In fact, we are delighted that you could make it home for Christmastide, the first time in a long time."

Stephen poured himself another port. "It is fortunate, but as it happens, I was summoned back to receive some information, which may necessitate me returning to the continent immediately after the festivities."

"I hope you will be able to stay to see in the New Year, Verity is planning a ball."

"Perhaps, it will depend on other factors," Stephen admitted.

"What factors?"

He leaned forward, considering before he spoke. "A document has fallen into our hands," he began.

"I imagine plenty of documents do that, I have calluses on my fingers from dealing with trading documents," Elliott said with a laugh. "All governments seem to delight in creating a mountain of documents."

"This one could very well affect the security of our country," Stephen said, quietly.

"Good God."

"Exactly."

"And you are the one to deal with this?"

"I am."

Elliott whistled. "I had suspected you were more than a diplomat, but this...." his voice trailed off. "Are you sure we should even be having this conversation?"

"Probably not," Stephen replied, "but you are my brother and an intelligent man." He paused. "There is something else, this document which cost lives before it came to me, is encoded. We know from what the last agent said that it concerns something to do with irrevocable change, but no-one in government service has been able to decipher it and given the possible incendiary contents we have not been able to bring in anyone from outside to do so."

"In which case, how do you know its contents are possibly incendiary?" Elliott asked.

"The man who delivered it to Whitehall was dead before he got to the end of the street. They tried to make it look as though he had been set upon by footpads, but there is no doubt that he was assassinated and should have been, presumably before he was able to deliver the document. He had the foresight to carry two versions of the document, so as far as we know, the people behind the document do not yet know it is in our hands."

There was a small cough from the doorway, and Stephen's gaze shot to the doorway.

"Verity wondered if you gentlemen were ready to join us," Ella said quietly.

Stephen stood up. "How much of the conversation did you hear?" he demanded.

"Enough," she said, coming further into the room. "Perhaps I might try to decipher your document," she said, boldly.

"That would be ridiculous," he replied. "If the best brains in government service cannot decipher it, what makes you think that you might? Quite apart from the fact that the whole matter is highly secret. You should not have been listening."

"You should not have been talking," she snapped..

"Touche," Elliott said quietly, adding, "why not let Ella have a look, she's something of a savant at enigmas, she keeps the children endlessly entertained making puzzles for them."

"I think you will find there is considerable difference between making puzzles for children to deciphering a highly sophisticated code," Stephen said, coldly.

"You insufferable man. Clearly it is better for you to keep it to yourself and risk whatever is in the document to occur than trust a woman to at least try to decipher it," she spat back, fury lighting the gold flecks in her eyes. She turned and strode out of the room, leaving the faint scent of lily of the valley in her wake.

Elliott whistled. "Congratulations. I thought I was an ass when Verity and I met again, but it was nothing compared to the pompous idiot you have just been. For your information, Ella is, some would say gifted in the field of mathematics, though she would never reveal it. I only found out when she came across a document of mine by chance and told me that one of my fellows was stealing small amounts and disguising the fact. The small amounts had built up to a sizeable amount by the time Ella looked and caught him and bearing in mind neither Burton, my secretary, nor I had noticed. As to this secret document, were she to see it, you know she would guard the secret with her life."

Stephen shook his head. "I had no idea about Ella's talents."

"Then I suggest two things. Firstly you apologise profusely for your attitude, secondly you ask for her help."

"And if that fails?"

"Beg."

Too angry to rest, Ella paced around her room. She had not gone to the drawing room after her spat with Stephen, but straight to her room. It did not take long for her maid to ready her for bed, but Ella knew she would not sleep. She tried reading but kept losing her place. Stephen Thorne was the most irritating, aggravating, infuriating man she had ever had the misfortune to meet, and he would be lucky if he survived the Christmas festivities without a stake of holly through his heart. Her murderous thoughts were interrupted by a knock on the door. "It is open," she called, "if that is you, Verity, I do not want to talk," she added. "I have nothing to say about that ridiculous, pompous fool, who is so full of his own self-importance I would be surprised his head could fit through a door."

"I'm afraid it is the pompous fool," a deep voice said from the doorway. "But I believe my head will fit," he said, coming into the room.

"What the devil are you doing here?" she demanded. "You should not be here. A gentleman should not enter a lady's bedchamber as you very well know."

"I have decided that you are no lady." *Damnation that did not come out as I intended.*

"I beg your pardon?"

"What I mean is that I am no longer going to treat you like a lady." *For God's sake Thorne, get a grip, every word that comes out of your mouth is putting a torch to the fire.*

"I think you had better leave now, Your Grace," Ella snapped, "before you say anything more insulting, though it would be hard to imagine what further insults you could possibly have in mind."

Stephen ran a hand through his hair. "I apologise, please Lady Ella, that is not what I meant at all."

"Then what did you mean?"

"I wanted to apologise for my behaviour and words earlier and ask if you would indeed be prepared to help me. If not for me, for the sake of king and country."

Ella looked at him in disbelief. "And what pray, brought about this rather sudden change of mind?" She was not going to make this easy for him.

"Elliott quite rightly pointed out that I was a fool to ignore the fact that you are someone who I would be able to trust with my life, as well as completely trustworthy with any secret, state or otherwise. He also explained that you are something of a mathematical genius and gifted in the way of ciphers and no-one but a complete idiot would turn down your offer to help," he explained. "Quite the testimonial," he added. "I know Elliott, his own standards are high and he is not a man to exaggerate, so if he tells me that you are the best chance of deciphering this document in a timely manner and you can be trusted, then I believe him."

"And how will your superiors respond when you tell them?" she asked.

"That will not be a problem, they are practical men and so long as the document is translated, they are unlikely to ask how and why. The important thing is to know what the document contains, so that we may make a plan of action to deal with what is inside. Please, Lady Ella, I humbly ask you, once again, to help me, many lives may very well depend on it."

Once more, Ella paused, was this not what she wanted, the chance to be something more than the spinster sister with a life restricted to the narrow confines of what society deemed appropriate for women of her station in life? Had she not said to Stephen earlier that she wanted at least one adventure before it became impossible? If she accepted this challenge it would be a great adventure, though she had no doubt that her part in the proceedings would be written out of history. History was full of the great doings of men, but women barely featured, not that she wanted recognition for herself, but it might bring to the minds of men the fact that women could be more than mere decoration. It would be a great responsibility, not just for advancing the cause of women, she hoped, but clearly it was vital for the good of the country. On the other hand, the work was secret so she doubted that anyone involved with it would be acknowledged in any way, and of course that was the right thing. But could she work with Stephen, who seemed determined to provoke her with every word he said? Time would tell.

"Very well," she said, taking a breath, "I will do what I can to help you, for the sake of the country and in the hope that you at least will see that women can work as well as men."

He came further into the room and took her hand. "Thank you."

Ella looked down to their joined hands, it was the first time Stephen had touched her without gloves and the feel of his skin on hers caused an interesting sensation. She quickly withdrew her hand. "Do you have the document with you?" she asked, stepping away from him. He suddenly seemed to be very large and very male in her feminine chamber.

"It is very late so I thought we might begin work on it early in the morning, shall we say seven o'clock? I will meet you in the library," he replied.

"Very well, though Christmas is close and I believe the children will demand at least some of our attention, in our roles as aunt and uncle."

"Of course, I would not dream of disappointing them as I have seen so little of them," he agreed.

"Until tomorrow then."

He turned to leave, but was stopped by her voice. "One more thing, the document, is it formed of letters or numbers?"

"Neither," he replied.

"Neither?" She raised her eyebrows. "Ciphers are usually one or the other or a combination of both."

"It is a most singular document, the likes of which I have never seen before, not as a secret document at least," he answered.

"Quite the puzzle then." For the first time since he had entered Swallowfield, she smiled.

CHAPTER 3

Somehow, he was not surprised to find Ella waiting for him when he entered the library the following morning. Neither was he surprised to find that she had cleared the large desk of almost all its contents, leaving only a magnifying glass, a pot of expensive graphite pencils and several equally expensive fresh sheets of paper. She sat behind the mahogany desk, lightly drumming her fingers on the leather writing surface.

"Good morning," he said, coming to a halt beside the desk. "You obviously broke your fast early."

"I found sleep difficult," she replied, "and I was not hungry. Do you have the document?"

He unrolled the paper and watched as Ella looked at it with surprise. "Is this a jest?" she asked, her eyes wide. She stood up. "I seem to find myself once more the recipient of your prejudice. Well done, Your Grace. I am sure when you relate the story to your cronies in Whitehall, they will be amused by your put down of the woman who thought she might be of some help in a man's world."

"Wait." He reached out and caught her hand. "Wait, please

Ella, that is not what I meant at all. This is the document. It is just that it is in a form no-one expected." It was the first time he had used her given name without her title and without permission, but somehow it felt right.

"It is a painting," she replied, looking at the watercolour. The scene depicted was pastoral, with two peasants resting against one of the trees that framed the piece with cows and sheep in the background. A stream ran through the foreground, and an open gate led the eye to the field beyond. There were hills in the distance with a small, ruined castle.

"Now mayhap you see why no-one has been able to unravel the meaning of this," he said, quietly.

Ella turned back to the painting. "Then I suppose we need to look at it more carefully."

"Could the two central figures represent someone, in government or at court perhaps?" she asked.

He shrugged. "It is possible, though to my knowledge, they do not resemble anyone with whom I am familiar."

"Could the fact that they are lounging against the tree, which is an oak, the symbol of England, perhaps represent the idle poor? Or the poor who are waiting for their moment to revolt?" She squinted at the picture again. "It could be that the group behind this cipher are a group of wealthy landowners who wish to return to the mediaeval days of peasants under the control of their masters."

"I doubt it, that would spark off a revolution such as the one in France."

"Mayhap that is their intention, to retain control of their own lands but remove those who make laws they find inconvenient."

Stephen thought for a moment. "I doubt wealthy, aristocratic landowners would take such a risk, especially when they consider what happened to their counterparts in Paris at the hands of Madame Guillotine."

Ella nodded. "Indeed. Once the cat is out of the bag, it is impossible to get it back in again."

"There is much fear of revolution in the country as it is, no-one surely would be mad enough to spark the tinder box and set it off. The aristocracy in this country has a talent for self-preservation," Stephen said with a wry grin.

Ella took a breath, when he smiled, Stephen was one of the most handsome men she had seen. The years fell away and she remembered the young man he had been when he had made his disastrous proposal. His eyes seemed to become an even darker blue framed by lush, dark lashes any woman would have envied. There were fine lines around his eyes, and deeper ones from his nose to his mouth suggesting that in the interim years, he had not led a life of idle pleasure. "Including you? Do you have a knack for self-preservation?"

"I certainly hope so," he laughed.

Ella lowered her eyes to the painting. It was the first time since they had met that the awkwardness between them had receded, and she liked it. Rather too much. She had to admit that she had always liked Stephen and as a young woman, had dreamed that he might offer for her, but when it came, she could not accept a man who would marry her out of pity and convenience. She still would not.

"The gate is open," she referred to the painting once again, she would not be distracted from the task by thoughts of what might have been. "The artist is encouraging our eyes to go through the gate, but where does it lead?"

"To that old ruin at the top of the hill?"

"Perhaps it is suggesting that landowners have had their day, that is why the castle is a ruin. Could it be that the workers have taken over and have set fire to the castle. Again, it would suggest some kind of revolution," she said.

"I suppose it is possible, after all, in France, many of the chateaux were razed to the ground."

"And yet the scene seems so peaceful."

"The calm after the storm?" he asked.

"There are storm clouds over the castle," she pointed out. "The question is, are they coming or going?"

"And the sheep and cows? Do they have a meaning? We cannot count every blade of grass and every leaf," Stephen said, "I think we are wasting our time."

"There," she exclaimed, pointing to the larger of the trees, "there, do you see it?"

"What? What do you see?" Stephen replied, leaning forward and peering at the scene.

"On the leaves," she said, picking up the magnifying glass. "On the leaves there are small numbers, facing in different directions, they are made to look as though they are the veins of the leaves, but there are definitely numbers," she added, her voice breathless with excitement.

"My God, so there are." He looked from the painting to Ella. "I would never have thought to look at that."

"That is because you were looking at the bigger picture and not at the details." She grinned. "You could not, in fact, see the wood for the trees." Her grin became a laugh. It was so infectious that he could not help but join in.

It was a moment to be cherished, for the first time since their awkward reintroduction, Ella had finally relaxed in his company, and he did not want it to end. He did not want Ella to retreat back into the hard, brittle shell she had built around herself, but he also knew that if he pushed, that would be exactly what would happen. Ella had lived so long under the shadow of her father's description of her as a 'monster' that she was unable to see herself as anything else.

"What now?" he asked, carefully schooling his features into a neutral expression.

"The numbers seem to be ordered into patterns, some three, some four and so on, which I assume means that they represent words." She bent over the paper.

"But how do we know where to start?"

"Well," she said as she straightened up, "when we are reading English text we begin at the top of the page and read from left to right, so I am going to start there." She pointed with the magnifying glass to the top of the largest tree in the foreground.

"Quite remarkable," he said.

"It is indeed" She turned her attention once more to the scene. "Using a picture to hide a code is extremely clever. One would never know to look if one did not know there was a hidden message to look for."

"What do you plan to do now?"

She cocked her head to one side. "I think the first thing is to note the numbers down on a clean sheet of paper, then I can begin to work out which letters they represent."

"May I be of assistance?" he asked.

She held out a pencil. "I rather think you may, if I read out the numbers, you might write them down, that way it will be quicker and I should be less likely to make a mistake. As you may imagine, a missing number could throw the whole thing out of balance."

"Of course, I shall be happy to assist you." He drew up a chair and sat beside her.

Two hours later, Ella rubbed the back of her neck. "I think that is all, certainly from the trees, though I shall have to look in greater detail at the rest of the picture to see if there are further clues hidden, but for now I think we both deserve a rest."

"I agree." Stephen placed the pencil on the desk and came to stand behind her. "Let me," he murmured, placing his hands on her shoulders and massaging them. "When I was in Greece a few years ago, I discovered that massaging a tight muscle works wonders."

Ella closed her eyes and sighed. "That does feel quite remarkable."

"Apparently the art of massage has been around for thousands of years, yet here we know little of it. I should wager that it does less harm than the leeches our physicians are so fond of." He applied a little more pressure, partly because he knew it would relieve her tension and partly because of all things, he wanted to feel her skin under his hands. He felt her tense. "Relax," he whispered, "trust me, this is the best thing for relieving tension." Another moment and he would kiss the bare skin of her neck.

Ella almost jumped, he was so close she could feel his breath on her neck, and she could feel delightful sensations spreading throughout her body.

"Thank you, Stephen," she said. "I feel much better now." She needed to tell him to stop before her brain stopped sensible thought.

Ella stood and quickly grasped the edge of the desk.

"What is wrong, Ella, are you ill?" he asked, his arm going out to steady her as she sank back onto her chair.

"I just felt a little faint," she replied, keeping her eyes closed as the room swam before her.

"Damnation, what were you thinking? It must have been hours since you ate." What was I thinking? He strode over and pulled the bell. "I'm so sorry Ella," he returned and knelt by her side, "I should have realised."

Fry, the butler, was quickly dispatched for tea and scones, while they waited, Stephen held Ella's hand and stroked stray strands of hair from her face. "You are very pale, my dear, but you will surely feel better when you have had some sustenance." As soon as the tea arrived, he insisted on pouring and holding a cup for her to sip from. He even broke small pieces of scone and fed them to her.

"Thank you," she said quietly. "I feel much better now." It had been a long time since someone had taken care of her and it felt dangerous. "I think some fresh air is probably what I need now."

"An excellent idea," Stephen replied. "I shall accompany you."

"There really is no need."

"Oh, there is every need." He smiled down at her. She may not need him, but he needed her.

CHAPTER 4

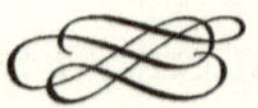

The air was crisp and cold. There had been an earlier sharp frost, but the weak sun had melted it so that it just remained in the areas the sun did not reach. Ella shivered a little and pulled her shawl closer, she was grateful for the woollen cap and gloves though the air nipped at her nose, and she had the impression that it had already gone red.

"I thought a walk to the lake," Stephen suggested, offering his arm.

"That would be nice," she replied. Whatever he had been doing since she last saw him had clearly involved physical activity as she could feel the muscles in his arm flex as she took it. "I wonder whether it is frozen, if so, I imagine Verity will want to organise some skating, she was very fond of it when we were girls."

"I doubt the ice will be thick enough in the middle at the moment, though if these frosts persist, I imagine the ice will be strong enough soon. Elliott is convinced we shall have snow within the week," he replied as they strolled along the gravel path towards the lake.

She smiled up at him. "The children will be delighted." Verity will no doubt have us all out here making snowmen, another thing we enjoyed as children, though we had to do it far away from the house so as not to annoy our father."

"Your father was not the kindest man I believe," he said, seriously.

"He was not, at best he was a troubled man, at worst he was something of a...well, I should not speak ill of the dead. He was my father for good or ill," she replied firmly. She pinned a smile on her face. "What about you, Duke? Did you make snowmen as boys?"

He looked into the distance. "Indeed, we did, though young boys are more into the habit of making snowballs and hurling them at each other than creating snowmen."

"You had another brother, other than Elliott?"

"Cameron was the eldest, he should have been the duke rather than myself," he said, starkly.

"I did not know. May I ask what happened if it is not too painful?"

He shrugged. "It was a long time ago. Cameron was several years older than Elliott and me, we were something of a late blessing, or so our mother said. Cameron went to the continent when we were just boys, while he was there, war broke out and we never heard from him again, he seemed to have just disappeared, his name never appeared in lists of the dead and no-one has any idea what became of him. After several years, father accepted that he was dead, and I was declared the heir. It broke our mother's heart and father was never the same after Cameron's disappearance."

"And you say no-one has ever confirmed your brother's death?"

He shook his head. "It is strange, but no-one seems to have any idea of what happened to him, we can only assume his death was one of many, lost in the fog of war."

"Was your brother in the military?" she asked.

"Not that I am aware," he replied, "though it is entirely possible that he may have joined a regiment out there. Our father's regiment, the Hussars were certainly present, but there is no record of Cameron having joined them."

"I am so sorry, not knowing what happened to your brother must in many ways be worse than knowing for certain he is dead," she said, squeezing his arm. "I am truly sorry."

He smiled down at her. "Thank you," he said, simply. "Elliott and I accepted a long time ago that we would probably never know what really happened to Cameron, but it would set our minds at ease if we could lay him to rest so to speak."

"I am surprised that no-one was able to confirm his death, it was not as though he was an insignificant individual, being the heir to a dukedom," she mused. "Unless of course...."

"Unless what?"

"Unless either no-one knew he was the son of a duke or he did not want anyone to know he was the son of a duke, if he was playing the part of an ordinary soldier, well, they did not keep lists and the men were, I believe buried where they fell," she finished. "Sorry, I was just thinking aloud, as Elliott told you, I have a fascination for puzzles of all kinds."

He pondered this. "No matter, in fact I find I am glad to be able to talk to someone about Cameron, our father could not bear to hear his name so Elliott and I stopped talking about him, though neither of us could ever forget our brother, it is as though we can neither mourn him nor give up hope that one day he will return to us."

"You would lose your dukedom," she pointed out.

"I should gain my brother, a far greater prize."

"Well, they do say that where there is hope, there is life," she responded. There were not many men who would consider losing their title and all the prestige that went with it, with such equanimity. She was beginning to warm to Stephen and that could be dangerous.

"I had not intended that we should descend into melancholy," he said. "Shall we take a turn around the lake and talk of more pleasant things?"

They walked on in companionable silence, the lake was at the end of the park, where the woodland began, the shade cast by the tall poplars and oaks had ensured that the ice had remained on the pond and the trees retained their lacy white shawls of frost. "Verity and I used to fish here when we were girls," Ella said, smiling at the memory. "Verity always managed to best me by catching the largest fish."

"And did you take them back to be cooked for your supper?"

"Of course not, the fun of angling was to catch the creatures, once we had judged who had won, we put them back. One particular trout was there for what seemed to us like years. We named him Toby because he reminded us of our old coachman."

"Toby the trout," he said with a laugh. "What other mischief I wonder, did the Grainger girls get up to?"

"Very little I assure you. This was not a house in which mischief was permitted," she said, the smile leaving her face and making Stephen wonder anew about the stories he had heard of her father.

They had almost circled the lake when they heard shouts and saw two small bodies hurtling towards the lake followed by the nursemaid.

Stephen's eyes narrowed. "She is never going to be able to catch up with them," he said, beginning to break into a run as the eldest, Lily ran, laughing onto the lake. "You can't catch me," she said, turning back and laughing towards the nursery maid.

"Stop," Ella screamed and caught the attention of the younger child who stopped, uncertainly, at the lake edge. Lily suddenly stood still in the centre of the lake. "It made a noise, the lake made a noise like when the coachman cracks his whip," she said.

"Lily," Stephen called out, taking off his greatcoat. "I want you to do just as I say, the first thing is to look at me. Now," he continued as the small girl looked at him with fear filled eyes, "I need you to lie down, that's all and I'll have you off in no time."

"Here," Ella said, tossing a branch towards him, "the ice will not bear Lily's weight, let alone yours. If you stay flat and push the branch towards her, she can hold it and you can pull her back."

Stephen nodded as he lay down and edged towards the child, pushing the branch in front of him. "Here, Lily," he said, keeping his voice as calm and cheerful as he could, "take hold of the branch with both hands if you can, and I will give you a ride back to the shore."

The small child stretched out her hands. "I cannot reach uncle, the branch is too far away," she cried.

"The ice is too thin for me to go further without the risk of it cracking and taking her under before I reach her," he said, quietly.

"I will do it," Ella replied. "I am lighter than you and if you were to hold my ankles, I should be able to reach her."

"Are you sure?" he asked.

"Quite sure," she said, dropping gently to her knees and beginning to slowly edge her way along the ice, pushing the branch in front of her. "Do not fret, Lily, see I am coming to help you and Uncle Stephen will make sure that we are both safe. Can you reach the branch yet?"

"Nearly," the child said, then gave a cry as the ice crackled again.

"I need to go further," she said over her shoulder.

"Keep your legs very straight and I shall push you," he said, keeping his voice calm as he took hold of her ankles and slowly pushed her towards Lily.

"There, can you grasp it now?" she asked, her whole body beginning to shake with tension.

She felt the branch quiver as her niece caught the tip of the branch. "I have it, Aunt Ella."

"Well done, now, hold onto it tightly," she said, "and your uncle can begin to pull us back to the shore."

For what seemed an age, Stephen pulled the woman and the girl back to the shore until Ella was able to stand and lift Lily safely into her arms.

"I'm sorry, your ladyship, the children were so excited when they saw you at the lake they ran, I slipped and couldn't catch them, thank goodness the youngest is in the nursery having their nap," the nursery maid said, wiping her eyes. "I shall hand in my notice directly."

"Nonsense, Nora is it not?" The young woman nodded. "There is no need for that and I am sure these two rascals have learned their lesson and fortunately, no real harm was done." Turning to her nephew and niece she added, "It is never safe to run onto ice, no matter how frozen it looks, you must always ensure that an adult is with you to test it first." Both children nodded solemnly. As if on cue, a large crack appeared and the ice split. The children's eyes followed the crack as it grew, "Sorry Aunt Ella," Lily said quietly.

"It is a good thing that we were here, thank goodness. Now off you go with Nora to get cleaned up and warm." She dropped a quick kiss on Lily's head and handed her back to the nursery maid.

"Come," Stephen held out his hand, "Lily is not the only one who needs to go inside and warm up." He gently placed his greatcoat around her shoulders, took her hands in his and chafed some warmth into them. "That was a brave thing to do," he said, looking into her eyes.

"I only did what you were about to do," she said, unable to tear her gaze from his.

"I can think of no other woman, except perhaps their mother, who would put her own life in danger as you just did," he said, softly. It would take the slightest movement, and she would be in his arms, and his lips would be on hers. Strange, he had proposed marriage to her, yet he had never kissed her, and it was the one thing, at this moment in time, that he wanted to do. Desperately.

CHAPTER 5

"Well, Lily doesn't seem any the worse for her ordeal. You know I shall never be able to thank you enough," Verity said later, as they watched the children playing on the rug with the wooden farm animals.

"I only did what anyone would do," Ella replied. "In fact, Stephen tried to, but we feared that the ice would not bear his weight." They both looked over to where the two men were playing on the floor with the children. "Stephen certainly seems to take his duties as uncle seriously," she added with a smile. He was currently mooing like a cow as he moved the animal from one 'field' to another.

"I cannot imagine there are many dukes of the realm who play with small children on the floor, and yet we have two of them," Verity said, adding, "he is a good man."

"I know that," her sister replied.

"I do not think his feelings towards you have changed," Verity ventured.

Ella turned towards her sister. "I know your wish is for Stephen and I to marry, but I must tell you now, Verity, there will be no wedding between us. What feelings Stephen once had for me were from a sense of duty to his title and pity for me, neither of which is a basis for a marriage, not the kind of marriage I should want. Oh, I know that women marry for far less, in order to secure position, comfort and some sort of protection, but the fact of the matter is that financially, although I could not claim to be a wealthy woman, I have sufficient for my needs so I have no need to tie myself to a man who does not love me. We both saw what happened to our mothers when they married without love, furthermore, I have seen the love that you and Elliott share and I am not willing to settle for less. That being said, I doubt it will ever happen so I have reconciled myself to being a spinster, indeed, at my age that is exactly what I am,"

Verity looked at her sister. "I understand, believe me, when I thought Elliott only wanted a marriage of convenience, I fought against it, but as you know, things turned out differently," she said with a smile, her eyes finding her husband across the room. "As for being a spinster, I would just say this. I have seen the way Stephen looks at you and it has nothing to do with pity or duty. Now," she called to her children, "it is time for bed. Your father will be along to read a story and I shall come and tuck you in." She raised an eyebrow towards her brother-in-law. "I trust I can count on you to behave as a gentleman, Stephen? As you know we do not necessarily hold to the chaperone rules here, and you are both old enough to behave sensibly."

He nodded and grinned. "Although not quite in my dotage, I shall endeavour not to besmirch Lady Ella's reputation."

Ella rolled her eyes.

"I cannot believe the amount of energy three small children create," Stephen said as he lowered his large frame into the chair opposite Ella. "I believe chasing around after a group of children would greatly improve the fitness of our military men, and a conversation with a three-year-old on the merits of ice cream for breakfast rather than bread and milk would tax the negotiation skills of our most senior diplomats."

"Since Elliott had the icehouse built, the children are all partial to as much ice cream as they can persuade their parents to let them have." Verity could not help but laugh. "I remember on one occasion last summer, they were given ices, Lily ate hers like a princess, none of it was wasted, or spilled, Francesca had a little on her chin and Teddy dived straight in, headfirst."

"That sounds like a boy after my own heart. Who would want bread and milk when they could have ice cream?"

"Who indeed?" Ella replied, laughing. For a moment, the years slipped away, and she remembered the conversations they had enjoyed so many years ago, when she had at last stepped out from the nightmare of her father's iron rule.

Sensing a change in mood he asked, "Now that you have the numerical code written down, what will you do next?" Talking about the task they had embarked upon seemed to enable Ella to relax.

"Each number clearly represents a letter, so it is a question of working out the sequence. Obviously the easiest would be that A equals 1, B equals 2, C equals 3 and so on, though I doubt that the person who encoded the message was so unimaginative."

He frowned. "There would appear to be a great deal of possible combinations."

"Very many, over a million I would say," she agreed.

"Then how on earth will you be able to find the right combination?"

She grinned. "There will be a pattern, it is just a case of working out what it is. That is the fascinating part. And yet," her expression changed, "I am conscious of the fact that this is not just any puzzle, do you really believe that there is some secret group fomenting revolution?"

Stephen looked into her eyes before answering. "Ever since the revolution in France and the loss of the American colonies, we suspect there has been a group of powerful men who are intent on removing the monarch and replacing him, not to improve the state of the country or the lives of the people, but one whom they could manipulate into doing what increases their wealth and power. Naturally, they would claim it would be for the benefit of the country, but that is just a ruse for them to get what they want. In order to do so they would have to manipulate the lower classes who feel they would have nothing to lose, to revolution, violent or otherwise, and history suggests that it would be violent."

"Good heavens, and you believe this document might reveal something of these plans?" Ella gasped.

He nodded. "It might reveal some names, places or plans. To be honest, though we have our suspicions, we have no real evidence of anything. That is why your work is of vital importance, and I cannot thank you enough for what you are doing."

"But what if..."

He leapt to his feet and took her hands in his. "Ella, are you quite well? You are as white as a sheet."

She looked into his eyes, biting her lip. "But what if I fail you? What if I cannot decipher the message? As you said yourself, this is not making up puzzles for the amusement of children. You have placed your trust in me, and it may be misplaced."

He released a hand as he reached forward and gently traced the outline of her cheek. "Ella," he said softly, "I have every confidence that you will be able to work your magic on the document as you have worked your magic on me." He drew her towards him and placed a soft kiss on her lips. Much as he wanted to deepen the kiss and take her fully in his arms to mould her soft curves to his hard body, he knew that she would pull away and that was the last thing he wanted. He moved back, her eyes fluttered open, he noticed the pulse beating at the base of her throat and smiled, Ella was not as immune to him as she believed herself to be.

"Why did you do that?" she asked, her voice, husky.

"To stop you from fretting about your perceived lack of ability," he replied, tucking an errant curl behind her ear. "And it worked."

"You promised Verity not to besmirch my reputation."

"It was only a kiss, Ella." And he had wanted to do so much more, he wanted to explore those inviting curves under her gown, he wanted to feel her nipples harden as he caressed them into buds. Much as she had tried to control it, he knew instinctively that Ella possessed a passionate nature and he wanted to be the one to unleash it.

"Of course, just a kiss," she responded with a small smile and turned away quickly so that he could not see the disappointment in her eyes. It was just a kiss, but it made her want things, things that she thought she had put behind her, she shook her head. "But kindly do me the courtesy of not doing so again, and I think it would be best if we returned to formal names," she said, tartly. She had to stamp out any intimacy with him before he insinuated himself into her heart again. It was just a kiss and meant nothing.

CHAPTER 6

Stephen could not sleep, every time his eyes closed, he was tormented by dreams of Ella, in his arms, slowly stripping the clothes from her body and seeing her naked perfection as he kissed and caressed every inch of her, feeling her beneath him when she cried his name as he made love to her, bringing them both to a shuddering climax. The final dream had him in a cold sweat as Ella disappeared under the ice of a huge lake and he could not get over its surface to rescue her. After what felt like hours tossing and turning and punching the pillow in frustration, he lit a candle and looked at his pocket watch, disappointed to find that it was only three o'clock and daybreak was hours away.

The decanter by his bedside held only water and he felt in need of something stronger if he was to get any rest, donning a banyan, he took the candlestick and made his way through the silent corridors to the library where he knew Elliott kept his best brandy. He had begun pouring a measure before he became aware of the light from the desk and Ella was so absorbed in what she was doing that she had not noticed him at all. She was sitting at the desk, her hair in a braid over one shoulder which was covered in a shawl over her nightrail. Her head was bent over what he assumed was the code they had written earlier, her pencil moving over the paper rapidly, making marks as it went. His mouth went dry when he noticed the tip of her pink tongue as she concentrated on what was in front of her.

"How long have you been here?" he asked quietly, moving towards her.

"Oh," she squeaked, her hand going to her heart. "You startled me. I did not know you were here."

"I apologise, for it was not my intention to frighten you."

"Of course," she replied, "I realise that, I was just unaware of your presence, Duke."

She had been serious about returning to formality, though at least she had not gone as far as addressing him as Your Grace, which she seemed to reserve for when she was angry with him. "I see that, my lady, you were clearly absorbed in whatever it is you were doing. May I ask if you have made some progress?"

"It is early days, but I believe I have." She smiled at him and the whole room seemed to light up.

He stepped nearer. "May I see?"

"Of course." She turned the page towards him.

There was a pause before he said, "Forgive me, but this makes little sense to me."

"I would not expect it to, but here," she turned the paper over. There were several grids each with a letter corresponding to a number.

"I have tried several combinations and it would appear that whoever constructed this cipher has not gone out of their way to make the actual code difficult, given the amount of trouble they went to in order to hide the code in the picture."

"Perhaps, having gone to so much trouble with the painting, they did not expect anyone to see that there was a code hidden there," he suggested.

"Exactly," she agreed.

He looked at her, as if seeing her for the first time. "But how did you come to link the numbers with the appropriate letters?"

"The most commonly used letter in the English language is e, so I looked for a number which recurred most frequently," she explained. "It is eleven."

He looked at the grid again. "A strange choice."

"Not really, the person who designed this code decided to start the alphabet at number seven."

"But what happened when he got beyond twenty-six, there are no higher numbers here?" He was beginning to feel like a dolt.

"He simply went back to one, see?" She pointed to the last grid on the page.

"But why begin at number seven?" he asked, puzzled. "It seems somewhat arbitrary."

"There are many who consider the number seven to be lucky," she replied. "Completely irrational in my opinion, but there again, many things that people do have no reference to logic or reason. A number is a number; it can be neither lucky nor unlucky and only is so by the value that people put upon it."

"I would have to agree, though there are many who hold to such superstitions, black cats crossing one's path, horseshoes and lucky rabbit's feet for example."

"Not so lucky for the rabbit," she replied.

"So now you have the corresponding letters you are able to translate it?"

She nodded. "It helps that our man was thoughtful enough to include punctuation, something I missed the first time I looked at the picture," she replied, picking up the magnifying glass and showing him the tiny marks on the leaves. "Though I should warn you that perhaps names and places may have been further obscured, that is what I should have done, had I written a coded message."

"You are quite remarkable Lady Ella." He smiled down at her, his hand itching to trace the delicate arch of her brow and down her cheek to her jaw before gently drawing her into his arms to kiss her, but she had made it quite clear that any intimacy between them was out of the question, and he would respect it, even if it killed him. "Though it is getting late and I think we should both retire to bed. We can work on it again on the morrow."

"You are right of course, but I doubt I shall be able to sleep. I have long found more than a few hours of slumber almost impossible, it is as though my mind fizzes with life the moment I close my eyes," she admitted.

"Then let us sit for a moment before the fire and have some of my brother's excellent brandy," he suggested. "I too sometimes find sleep eludes me." He moved towards the fireplace and poked the embers into life before throwing another log on it. Then offered her a glass. "Come, sit and warm yourself."

"I have never tried brandy, Father always kept a fine cellar but would not allow us to drink anything other than lemonade. He said anything else would be wasted on silly girls," she replied, taking a sip and coughing as the liquid hit the back of her throat. "My goodness," she wheezed, "I see now something of Father's point. I cannot imagine why so many gentlemen find it pleasing to drink."

"Practise," he said, smiling. "I promise you the next sip will be both warming and more pleasant."

"So Duke, what is it that keeps you from slumber?" she asked.

You. "Any number of things, working for the government can be a lonely business, there are few who are able to both share and understand the experience." He stopped suddenly, as he had not intended to reveal so much.

"I had not considered the solitary nature of the work you do," she mused, twirling a lock of hair around her finger. "The greatest secret I am usually called upon to keep are those regarding who is to wear what at some ball or other."

"I imagine you would be thrown in the tower were you to divulge this highly inflammatory information to the wrong person," he teased.

"Oh, much worse," she replied. "I should be given the cut direct in every ballroom in London and have to retire to the country until I was forgiven, if I ever was forgiven."

"It makes the keeping of state secrets seem quite dull by comparison," he answered, smiling down at her, marvelling at how right their situation felt. She returned his smile and tucked her feet beneath her.

"Are you cold?" he asked.

"A little." She pulled her shawl a little tighter. "I had not noticed the room getting cold."

He reached across to the adjacent chair and retrieved a blanket. "Here," he said, tucking it around her.

"You must share it, for I believe that you are equally as cold as I."

To be honest he was feeling the cold, his banyan was designed for warmer climes, and he had little on beneath it other than his breeches. "Very well," he agreed, moving closer towards her, scandalously close, so that he could feel the shape of her thighs against his own. It seemed the most natural thing in the world to put his arm around her and draw her close. "Friends," he said, when she started. "Friends sharing a little warmth. There is surely no harm in that." To his surprise, she did not protest and leaned her head against his shoulder. "Friends," she agreed.

The fire had turned to embers and dawn was breaking when he woke up, Ella was still sleeping against his shoulder. It was strange, both of them had admitted that they found sleep elusive, and yet this night they had both slept. It had felt right to have her so close to him. He was reluctant to wake her, but he knew that the servants would be rising and soon the house would become a hive of activity as fires were lit and water was heated.

"Ella," he whispered against her hair. "Ella, it is time to wake up."

"I do not want to," she mumbled, sleepily, snuggling against him.

"Neither do I," he replied, dropping a gentle kiss on her hair, "but the household will be coming to life shortly and I do not think your sister would approve of us snuggled up here like a pair of turtledoves."

She sat up quickly. "Oh, my goodness, we must not be found here together."

"Exactly, you run up to your bedchamber and try to catch the last remnants of sleep. I shall stay here. Elliott would not find it at all unusual that I repaired to the library in the night to partake of his brandy and fell asleep."

"What of the documents?" she asked, her eyes straying to the desk.

"I shall lock them in the drawer until you return," he replied. "And Ella," he added as she rose, "I shall expect to see you in the breakfast room, partaking of a hearty breakfast. We have much to do and I do not want to see you faint from lack of nourishment."

She rolled her eyes.

"I have noticed you do that," he said quietly. "It certainly has an effect, though I doubt it is the one you intend."

"What sort of effect?" she could not help but ask.

"This," he replied, pulling her into his arms and lowering his head. From the moment it started the kiss was explosive, this was no gentle meeting of the lips. He urged her lips to part with his tongue and delved inside when she opened for him. Their tongues intertwined as he pulled her closer, wanting to feel every inch of her softness against his hard body, wanting her to feel what she did to him. Just wanting her. His eyes almost opened with surprise when she did not pull away but put her arms around his neck and pulled him closer. She wanted him, the question was, would she ever admit it either to herself or him? It was a question he was determined to answer before this Christmastide was over.

CHAPTER 7

Ella did not know how she managed to get back to her chamber, her legs felt as though they were filled with water and her heart seemed to be beating at twice its normal rate. Try as she might to ignore the attraction between them, she could not deny that he had an effect on her that no other man had and if she was not vigilant, he would wear down her defences and where would that lead? To heartbreak. If she gave in to the attraction she felt for him, it would ruin the fragile understanding they had reached. And what then? He would be gone, no doubt from the country and she would be just a memory, if he ever thought of her at all. No, she must ensure that there was nothing between them other than friendship, she could live with that. And when she had done her duty and deciphered the document, he would go on his way and she would, no doubt go back to her small life but with the knowledge that something she had done had made a difference.

Stephen swirled the amber liquid around before taking a sip and grimacing. Drinking before breakfast, that is what you have reduced me to Ella Grainger. There was something between them, an attraction he could feel, she responded to him even though she fought against it, but it was as though she was made for him. The trouble was her father, he had derided and belittled her to the point that she had built a wall so high around her feelings that it was almost impossible to breach. But breach it he would, if it took him the rest of his life, though he did not want to waste another single minute without her in his bed and his heart. He would take that wall down brick by brick until she realised that not only was she worthy of love, but she was already loved. After this assignment was finished, he would, he decided, resign his position. The life of a diplomat, or at least the kind of diplomat he was, was lonely and dangerous. It was a long time since he had considered the danger as merely thrilling, and although he would always serve his country when called, what he desired now was to spend time tending to his estates and being the duke his tenants needed him to be. If he had to travel, it would be to take Ella to the places she wished to see, so that he could see them through her eyes.

Ella was already in the breakfast room nibbling a piece of toast when Stephen entered. "I sincerely hope you are having more than that," he said, helping himself to a hearty serving of bacon, eggs, mushrooms and tomatoes from the chafing dishes on the sideboard.

She rolled her eyes and quickly looked away, remembering what happened the last time.

"Hmm," a voice said, quietly, dangerously close to her ear. "I do not believe you learned your lesson regarding the eye-rolling."

"I think I shall go to the library," she said, rising quickly and turning her face so that he could not see the blush on her cheeks. A quiet chuckle followed her.

Stephen did not immediately follow her; he was just finishing his coffee when Verity entered. "Ah, Stephen, I was hoping to catch you," she said, sitting down next to him. "I wanted to talk to you about you and Ella."

"There is no Ella and I," he replied.

"But you would like there to be?" She raised an eyebrow.

"You know I offered for her, years ago, she does not want me, she has made that abundantly clear," he muttered.

"Ella has her pride, she believed and still does, that you were proposing out of pity, that you were settling for a wife you did not and probably would never love but who would provide you with an heir and that she would be so grateful that any man would have her that she would fall at your feet with gratitude. Do I have the right of it?"

"That was not how I felt, but now you put it like that I see that my reasons were not clear," he admitted.

Verity shook her head. "You must understand that Ella has suffered much. Firstly, from our father who did not hide his revulsion from her and, when she was allowed out, the taunts and slights she suffered from members of the ton who base their judgements of women solely on their attractiveness. I fear she has built a wall around herself that even the most ardent suitor would struggle to overcome."

"The scars are all but gone," he replied, knowing exactly to what Verity was referring.

"The physical scars of course," she agreed. "But the mental scars remain, I think that when Ella looks in the looking glass, she sees the scars as though they were inflicted only yesterday, even, as you say, they have faded to be barely visible," she paused. "Please do not hurt my sister."

"I would never want to hurt Ella," but she has made it clear that all she wants from me is friendship."

"Then be her friend." Verity smiled at him. "She needs a good friend."

When he entered the library, she was leaning over the desk, giving him the most charming view of her pert derriere.

"Peterloo," she said quietly.

"What about Peterloo?" he asked, coming into the room and standing beside her.

She pointed to a piece of paper. "It is mentioned here. We must not make the mistakes of Peterloo.'"

"Does it say whether they are the mistakes of the authorities or of the people?" he asked, sharply.

"I am not sure, but I suspect it is on the side of the authorities, there is something about 'the charge must be led by the lower classes to distract... I am sorry, I am still working on the next part, but it sounds as though...."

"What?" he prompted.

"It sounds as though either the revolution is to be led by the poor, or the poor are to be used as a distraction so that the powerful men behind this can carry out well, I can only call it treason."

His eyebrows rose. "Treason?"

"There is something else, something about removing the current usurpers and here, see." She pointed to a line further down the page "Restoring a true Tudor to the throne." She looked up at him. "How can that be? Queen Elizabeth died childless, that is why the Stuarts came to the throne and when Queen Anne died, George of Hanover came to rule. The idea is preposterous."

"Dear God." He ran a hand through his hair.

"What? They are our most recent royal houses are they not?"

He nodded. "They are."

"Then why are you looking as though you are about to be taken to the Tower of London?"

Stephen took a breath. "There is a story, a myth really, that Queen Elizabeth, Good Queen Bess was married in secret to Dudley, Earl of Leicester and that she had a child, a son who was spirited away to be raised in secret and safety."

"But that is impossible," Ella exclaimed. "She was the Virgin Queen, and such a thing could never have remained secret."

He shrugged. "It matters not whether it is true, the fact is, there are a group of people, powerful people who wish it to be true and therefore believe it to be true. Not only that, they believe that this child went on to live and procreate and there is an heir alive to this day who is the rightful ruler of this nation. And if they do not in fact believe this moonshine, it is a powerful tale they can use to their advantage to exploit those who would do away with the House of Hanover."

Ella considered for a moment. "And you believe that these people wish to provoke a revolution so that they may place this so-called Tudor heir on the throne."

He nodded. "I believe it is possible that there are some who are disgruntled with the House of Hanover, some who have not prospered under its rule, who wish to stir up the masses against them and replace the king with a puppet whom they can manipulate to their advantage. To do it, they will need the populace to revolt by whipping up any grievances they have about the price of bread, wages, the right to vote, any number of things in fact. Once the populace becomes a mob, who knows what will happen?"

"Those who want change will no doubt blame all their ills on the king and the mob will bay for his blood, as they did in France," she mused.

"Indeed. Though, those in power will surely have learned the lesson of revolution, in that once the beast tastes blood it demands more and more. The leaders of the revolution were in their turn consumed by the blood lust that followed, the Reign of Terror."

"And you think that there are people in this country who are plotting the same thing here? A revolution?" Her eyes were wide.

He nodded. "I think it is possible, this document is only one part of the information that has come into our hands."

She put her hand over her heart. "But that would mean a civil war".

"Exactly, such as we had almost two hundred years ago, from which it took many years to recover, and there are parts of the country which have not yet fully recovered. We may not like our system or indeed the House of Hanover, but what they represent is stability, there can be no progress without it and we are entering a period of great change, industrialization is changing the face and nature of the country and if we are at war with each other we will not be able to take advantage of the opportunities the new technologies we are developing which will, in turn cause us to lag behind and create greater poverty and disenchantment."

"Surely though, the poor have nothing to lose in changing the system. They have no land, no property, it matters little to them who sits on the throne if they do not have enough bread to feed their children," she responded.

"Of course, and that is precisely what these men intend to capitalise on. They will present their alternative as though it will be the answer to all the problems of the poor, then they will rouse them to violence with seditious speeches and, in the chaos that ensues, they will take power."

"But if they have promised to improve the lot of the poor, I can see why the poor would willingly follow them," she countered.

He shook his head. "These men have no intention of improving the lot of the poor, if that is what they desired to do, they could do it already. These are men who already hold many of the levers of power, they could pay their workers better, they could build better houses and schools as well as look after the old and infirm. They already have the means to do this, but they choose to look the other way, because they do not care. What they do care about is seizing power and gaining as much wealth as they can. The promises they make for reform will come to naught. We shall be left with the ruins of a country; the rich will get richer and the poor will get poorer."

"And what of this tale of Queen Elizabeth? Do you believe it?"

He shrugged. "It matters not if I believe it, and I do not. But if they can persuade enough of the populace to believe it and focus their dissatisfaction against the king, they will have their revolution."

CHAPTER 8

Ella sat down before her legs gave way. "When I awoke this morning, the world seemed quite normal, now I do not know what to think," she murmured. "On the surface, everything is as it should be, but underneath nothing is right. Suppose, just suppose, that this Tudor claimant to the throne exists, had the original heir been recognised, our history would have been completely different. There would have been no civil war."

"Perhaps," he answered. "On the other hand, there were enough nobles who wanted the wealth of the church for themselves. In any case, there were many who did not approve of Dudley and would never have allowed his family to influence the crown, that is one of the reasons that the Queen never married, had she allied herself with the Dudleys, she would have been removed. Times were harsh and uncertain to say the least, look at what happened to poor Lady Jane Grey."

"The one who ruled for only nine days before losing her head?"

"Precisely, they were ruthless men then and there are ruthless men now."

"The castle," Ella exclaimed.

"The what?"

"The castle in the picture, I knew I knew it from somewhere." She leapt up and searched the shelves until she found the book she was looking for. Having placed it on the desk, she leafed through it quickly. "There," she pointed to an illustration. "Nottingham castle, well the remains of it are exactly the same as the one in the picture."

"I suppose the artist had to use something to base his depiction on."

"Do you not see? Nottingham castle was occupied by the supporters of King John and when his brother King Richard returned, he besieged the castle and put down the rebellion." She paused, looking for some clue that Stephen knew what she was talking about. "The usurper was defeated by the rightful king. Do you not see the similarities with the coming of this possibly true Tudor heir to the throne?"

Stephen's eyes narrowed. "And the current owner has moved out of the ducal mansion since Nottingham is no longer a picturesque market town but has the worst slums in the country since the industrialization of the town. So the poor of Nottingham would be primed and ready for revolution. Though I imagine there must be some kind of final meeting among the conspirators before their plan is set in motion."

"Exactly. All we need to do is find, somewhere in the picture, the clue that is the key to when this revolution will begin, and then we can stop it before blood is shed."

Stephen looked up sharply. "What do you mean 'we'? There is no way on God's green earth that you will be doing any of the stopping. These are dangerous people, and they will not take kindly to their plans being thwarted. It will be dangerous and, I imagine, violent. This is not the sort of work for a woman."

"But surely," she began.

"But nothing Ella, you have been invaluable in deciphering

the coded message, and for that I and the country will be forever grateful. But, even if we were to find where the conspirators are to meet, you will not be a part of it." He paused. "Ella, are you listening to me?"

"Of course," she replied absently, her eyes focussing once more on the image.

"Did you hear that I just said that the moon is made of green cheese?"

"Most definitely," she replied.

"Ella, what is it you see?"

She looked up and gave him a knowing smile. "I think I know when and where this final meeting will be."

"And?" he prompted, adding, at her hesitation, "I surely do not need to tell you how important this information is, and how there is no time to lose."

"You do not."

He clenched his jaw, nearly grinding his teeth. "Then would you do the courtesy of telling me what it is?"

"I will not." She smiled..

"Ella, this is no time to play games."

"I assure you I have no intention of playing games. I shall give you the information once you have promised, nay sworn that I will accompany you to the meeting."

"You are behaving like a child, and this is man's work," he ground out, barely able to resist shaking some sense into her.

"I think you will find that another pair of eyes and ears, female eyes and ears will be helpful, especially in the form that the final meeting is to take place," she replied.

"What the devil are you talking about?"

"Your word, Stephen."

His long legs quickly covered the distance between them, and he placed his hands on her shoulders. "Ella," his voice softened, "do not ask this of me. What if things were to go wrong, badly wrong? I have had comrades who did not come back from such missions. If we are found out, there is no telling what might happen, these men will have no hesitation in torturing you to find out what you know before killing you. I cannot let that happen, Verity would never forgive me, and I would never forgive myself."

Ella leaned her head back so that she could look into his eyes, quite the darkest blue eyes she had ever seen. "I thank you for your concern, Stephen, but I assure you that I am quite able to rise to the challenge."

"I know you think you are but...aargh."

Quite how it happened, Stephen was unable to say, one moment he had Ella firmly in his grasp and the next, he was on the floor, his hands held behind his back with Ella sitting on top of him, his nose less than an inch from the expensive Aubusson carpet.

"I think," a voice said in his ear, "this answers the question of whether I am up to the challenge. And," she added, slightly tightening her grip, "if you struggle, you may find that your shoulder sort of pops out. It is, I am told, extremely painful."

"What the hell?" was all he could manage.

"It is a kind of Chinese, what they call martial art," she explained. "Elliott arranged for Verity and I to have lessons after her kidnap. Verity was happy to learn the basics, but I enjoyed it more and studied further."

"And how did Elliott come across this?" he grunted.

"There were two Chinese sailors on one of his trading ships, on one of the voyages, they gave a sort of exhibition fight and Elliott was intrigued. After Verity was abducted, he thought it would be a good idea if we could defend ourselves and invited Mr. Chen to teach us. A handy skill do you not think?"

She loosened her grip and allowed him to sit up, within a second, she was on her back with both her hands caught in one of his as he straddled her.

"Handy indeed, but here is another lesson, never underestimate the cunning or desperation of your opponent."

"That was not fair, Stephen, and were I in a situation where you were a real threat, I should not have relaxed my hold on you."

"That is the trouble Ella, you do seem to have a hold on me," he said as he lowered his head to hers and captured her lips in a kiss. When he ran his tongue along her lips, her mouth opened and his tongue delved inside. As she moved restlessly beneath him, he released her hands, but instead of pushing him away as he expected, she placed them on either side of his head and kissed him back. He relaxed, it felt so good to have her soft, pliant body beneath him, the trouble was, it was not enough, he wanted her naked and writhing beneath him as he pleasured her.

Suddenly, the pliant body stiffened and once again, he was underneath her, on his back this time, his arms pinned to his sides by her thighs. "Well," he grinned, "If that is the way you like it Ella, I shall be only too happy to oblige."

She leapt off him as though he were a tiger about to pounce. "You still have not given your word," was all she said.

"I am still not happy about involving you in this," he ground out, standing up and dusting himself off.

"Very well." She turned to go.

"Wait," he said. "You understand that what we may meet will be violent, dangerous and dirty, these people do not play by any rules, if you stand in their way, they will remove you by any means?"

"I understand."

"And will you promise that if I tell you to flee, you will flee?"

"I will."

"Without argument?"

She screwed up her face. "I cannot promise that."

"Without argument?" he persisted.

"Oh, very well, without argument," she conceded.

"In which case, I reluctantly agree to you coming on the mission."

"Thank you, though it would have been simpler had you agreed to my terms in the first place," she huffed.

"Now, when and where is this meeting to take place?"

"Oh, I do not know, just yet," she replied airily. "But I know where to look and I shall have the whole document ready for you in a day or two. In the meantime, I suggest that we enjoy Christmastide," she said as she sauntered from the room.

Stephen watched her pert derriere sway as she left, I am either going to strangle her myself or take her to my bed and never let her leave, he thought as he helped himself to his brother's best brandy. Either way, that woman is going to be the death of me. But he conceded, he now had a healthy respect, not only for her intellectual prowess, but now knew she could floor a man almost twice her size, that had come as something of a surprise, perhaps he could get her to teach him some of what she knew regarding this martial art as she had called it. He grinned to himself, it would be a painful experience no doubt and Ella would thoroughly enjoy it, whether he would was a moot point.

CHAPTER 9

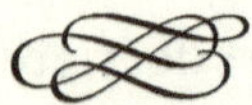

"There is nothing quite like sitting in front of a roaring fire, having had a good dinner and enjoying watching the children play with their new gifts," Verity said to her sister as they enjoyed a cup of tea whilst the men were at their port. "I am so glad that you and Stephen were able to join us this year, the children have loved having their aunt and uncle to play with."

"And we have not killed each other....yet," Ella said with a grin.

"Do I detect something of a thawing in your relationship with Stephen?" Verity asked, watching her sister closely.

"Perhaps, though do not make more of it than there is. Stephen and I have agreed to be friends, that is all."

Verity raised a delicately arched eyebrow, "Stephen is it?"

"That is his given name is it not?"

Verity shook her head. "Why do I get the feeling there is more to this story than you are telling me?"

"When there is something to tell, believe me you will be the first to know," Ella assured her sister, marvelling at how easily the lie tripped off her tongue.

"Now that is a sight for sore eyes," Elliott announced as he entered the room, "my two favourite women. Are they not beautiful brother?" He nudged Stephen.

"We are indeed blessed," his brother agreed.

Verity giggled and Ella rolled her eyes.

"Come, Verity." Elliott pulled his wife to her feet. "It is Christmas night and I have a desire to hear you play some carols." He led her to the pianoforte and sat beside her, singing in a rich baritone, if slightly out of tune as she played his favourite, 'Hark the Herald Angels Sing.'

"I see you have still not learned to curb your habit of rolling your eyes, most reckless." Stephen was so close she felt his warm breath on the back of her neck.

"There is, as far as I am aware, no law against it," she replied, pertly.

He chuckled, the sound now in his throat. "No law except perhaps the law of unexpected consequences."

He sat down beside her. "I have to ask, have you made more progress with the document?"

"I have," she answered.

"Will you share the information with me? No games please, Ella, there will be arrangements that need to be put in place."

"I had no intention of keeping the information from you, I worked on it last night."

"Then meet me in the library when Elliott and Verity have retired," he said quietly.

Apart from the creaks of the house settling, all was quiet as Ella made her way down the stairs to the library and she was not surprised to see candlelight coming from under the door.

Stephen was already sitting at the desk looking at the painting when she entered.

"Here," she held out the key to the desk drawer. "I thought it best to lock things away, just in case."

He placed the papers on the desk and began to read:

For all true red blooded English noblemen, the time to act is now. For too long we have been ruled by those whose reign we did not choose. They have failed the nation, wealth, wars and colonies have been lost and we must rise up and say 'no more.'

The lower classes must be made to act, for while our mealy-mouthed politicians and those who would thwart our aims are quelling the mob, we shall take control and bring back the true and rightful heir of the House of Tudor to the throne, who will reign with our will and guidance. The boy king will be crowned in Westminster Abbey before Midsummer Night. Once the revolt is complete, we shall disperse the mob and the power to govern will be where it should rightfully be, with men of land and title. Those nobles and any who resist will be stripped of their wealth and titles and hanged as traitors, such examples mollified the mob in France and will do the same here. If the mob does not disperse, the militia will deal with them. We must not make the mistakes of Peterloo.

Those who wish to join our noble endeavour must attend a masked ball at Bolton Castle on St. Valentine's Day. Death to traitors of the cause.

Stephen released a long breath. "My God, so it really is true. There is a plot."

"There is more but I thought it best not to commit it to paper," she replied. "Apparently the invitations to the ball will go out to all men of substance by Twelfth Night. You will probably receive one, during the ball, those men who wish to join the insurrection will be taken down to the secret tunnels to swear allegiance to the cause. To the rest of the party, it will just appear to be a masked ball. Quite how they will learn who is with them is unclear. Perhaps there will be another encoded message."

"I must send word of our success to Sir Robert." He rose.

Ella placed her hand on his arm. "I know you have not solicited my opinion, but I shall risk it. I believe that any communication with your superiors risks the perpetrators finding out what you know."

"Go on."

"Any communication, especially a written one, carries the risk of it falling in the wrong hands. Who is not to say that these conspirators are not watching this house, knowing that you have their document? I trust the staff here implicitly; there are perhaps some in the village who would be tempted by the right amount of coin. Then there is the risk of the messenger, either being corrupted or attacked and even the office could have been infiltrated by the group. Until we know more about this group, I advise that we proceed with caution."

He sat down and ran a hand through his hair. "I believe you are right. We do not know how far this corruption has gone and until we do..."

"There are just the two of us," she finished for him.

He looked at her steadily. "I am still not comfortable with your involvement in this."

She nodded. "I know, but I cannot let you shoulder this burden on your own. It will be more of an adventure than I had imagined." She risked a small grin. "At least we have some time to plan our approach."

"Very well." He sighed. "It would appear that whatever I might say, you are determined to play a part in what transpires."

"I am," she replied.

He looked thoughtful. "What was their purpose I wonder, in portraying Nottingham Castle when their true meeting place was to be Bolton Castle?"

She shook her head. "Perhaps as a ruse to put anyone off the scent, or perhaps just a coincidence or perhaps the one who devised the message has some connection with it, but the message is quite clear, the time and place St. Valentine's Day at Bolton Castle."

"Then what, if anything, do you know of this Bolton Castle?"

"As it happens, quite a lot," she answered. "It is in the riding of North Yorkshire and near where my Aunt Bette's husband, Sir Thomas has an estate which he primarily uses for hunting. It is where Mary, Queen of Scots was detained for six months after her escape from Scotland. Although much of it was ruined in the Civil War, a great deal of it is still intact and there are little known tunnels and caverns beneath it, hence a sensible choice for both the ball and the nefarious purpose of recruiting fellow conspirators."

"You sound as though you know it quite well."

She nodded. "I went with Aunt Bette, and we were shown around by the Earl of Bolton, who I assume is one of the conspirators?"

Stephen shook his head. "It is possible, even likely, though it may be that he has been duped into holding this ball and is completely innocent of what is to happen beneath his feet, so to speak. If he knows nothing of the meeting, he can say nothing when he is questioned. Though I have to say the possibility of him being entirely innocent of the whole thing is somewhat remote."

Ella pursed her lips. "Could it be that he thinks he is hosting something similar to the 'Hellfire Club'? Although notorious, I do not believe it is where revolution is plotted."

Stephen could not help but grin. "And what do you know of the Hellfire Club, it is not the sort of thing that an innocent maiden should know about?"

"I am inwardly rolling my eyes," she said, impishly. "It is rumoured that the Hellfire Club is more a place for pleasures of the flesh to be enjoyed, banquets served by scantily clad or naked women, that sort of thing."

The grin became a laugh. "I think the name gives it more notoriety than it deserves. It is true that dinner is served, though it is almost always cold by the time it reaches the diners and there are women who serve it though they would probably die of cold if they were scantily clad. There is talk of politics and sport as men are wont to do when they are together, but the tales of debauchery are much exaggerated."

Ella's eyes widened. "You mean to say that you have been to the Hellfire Club?"

He arranged his face as best he could in a neutral expression. "I could not possibly say, my lady."

"I believe, duke, that you are quite incorrigible."

"I certainly hope so." He laughed again.

It was good to return to a semblance at least of the easy way they had once been with each other.

"How would you like to go for a ride?" Stephen asked. "The threatened snow has not materialised and I for one could do with blowing away some of the cobwebs after a few nights of eating and drinking."

"I should like that," Ella replied. "I imagine the horses too are ready for some exercise."

"Then I suggest we both try to get some sleep in what is left of this night."

Ella nodded. "I doubt I shall sleep much but I shall try." She paused. "Of all the things I expected, this Christmastide has been one of the strangest."

Stephen quirked an eyebrow, "Only one of the strangest?"

Ella tilted her head and laughed. "You know what I mean. When I arrived, I thought I would have a quiet family Christmas, I did not imagine that I should be involved with such clandestine activities."

"Nor did I imagine that I should acquire a brilliant and beautiful assistant."

"Who can toss you on your arse if you displease her," she exclaimed with a laugh as she exited the room.

"What the hell have I let myself in for?" Stephen muttered to himself but could not help the grin spreading across his face. At last, after six long years, his relationship with Ella was approaching the way it once was, and he fully intended to take advantage of the time they would be spending together to make her realise that they were well suited. His grin faded, if they both survived.

CHAPTER 10

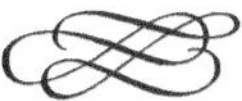

As she had expected, Ella was unable to sleep but even so, she found Stephen waiting for her when she entered the stables.

His eyebrows rose. "Are you planning on riding astride?" he asked, taking in the close-fitting trousers, jacket and highly polished boots. The only concession to a feminine riding habit was the jaunty dark green velvet hat perched on her head.

"There are some who believe that if a woman rides astride, her womb will somehow fall out. I assure you that riding side-saddle is more likely to result in her brains falling out when she hits the ground, having fallen from her horse because, unlike riding astride, she is unable to maintain a grip on the horse. However," she continued, "should you wish to put my theory to the test, feel free to ride Beautiful here, who, despite her looks, has been trained to work with regular and side-saddles. In fact, I should like to see all men attempt to ride side-saddle, then we should no doubt be rid of this nonsense."

"Surely riding side-saddle cannot be so difficult, after all hundreds, if not thousands of women have been riding like that for many years." The words were barely out of his mouth before he realised he had been manipulated.

Ella could not suppress a grin. "Very well, let us go to the schooling ring and you shall be able to show me exactly how easy it is."

Five minutes later, Ella perched on the fence as Stephen faced his first challenge of mounting Beautiful who had decided that she was not going to cooperate.

"Your left foot goes into the stirrup with your left leg anchored under the leaping head, and your right leg hooks around the fixed head," she provided, helpfully.

"What the devil are you talking about?" he asked, from the mounting block.

"The two pommels, the top one is the fixed head, and the bottom one is the leaping head," she said.

"This is bloody ridiculous," he muttered as he threw his leg over the horse. His foot was barely in the stirrup when Beautiful started to move.

"Good God," he said, bouncing in the seat.

"Use your right leg for balance and keep your left foot rigid," she advised. "Now are you ready to trot?"

"I do not think so," he replied.

"Unfortunately, it would seem that Beautiful is," Ella remarked as the horse broke into a smart trot.

It was with horror that Ella saw Beautiful's intention, there was a small jump at the back of the ring, a jump that, were he to be riding astride, Stephen would barely have noticed, but as he bounced and jolted in the side saddle, she knew it would be a disaster.

"Look out," she cried. She quickly jumped off the fence and ran towards the jump to see Beautiful and Stephen part company as the horse sailed over the fence and Stephen lay in a motionless heap in front of it.

"Oh my God, Stephen. Are you all right?" she said as she knelt down beside him. "I'll never forgive myself; I should never have goaded you. Please, please be all right." Her hands ran over his body, checking for broken bones.

"If you carry on Ella, you will very soon find I am more than all right," an amused voice interrupted her ministrations.

She snatched her hands away. "Thank God, if anything had happened to you I doubt Elliott would ever forgive me."

He sat up. "So your only concern was for Elliott's reaction?"

She bit her lip. "Not entirely," she admitted. The thought of Stephen being injured had caused what she could only describe as panic. "I think Verity would have something to say about me breaking her guest as well," she added, impishly.

"Minx," he said, holding out a hand. The minute she took his hand she knew it was a mistake, skin to skin was dangerous, she could feel the calluses on his fingers, a duke he may be, but he clearly did not lead an idle life. It felt as though the warmth of his hands shot through her palm and entered her, making her aware of him with every part of her body, especially her most feminine parts. This would not do, they were colleagues, friends at best and they had difficult and dangerous work ahead of them. She could not allow any attraction to develop because, she admitted to herself, that she was attracted to Stephen, she always had been, but his offer of marriage had killed any dream that she had that he might love her and she would not marry a man for convenience. She had seen her father's marriages of convenience, and she had seen her sister's love match, and she knew which she wanted, though her hopes of a marriage of any kind had long been dashed.

"I find myself wondering what thoughts are going on behind that expressive face of yours," Stephen said, softly. They were standing only inches away from each other, her small hand still in his, and it would take only the slightest movement for her to be in his arms.

"Nothing really," she lied. "I was thinking...."

Her words were cut off as Beautiful came over and nudged her shoulder.

She laughed as the horse nuzzled her. "I think Beautiful wants to go for a ride."

"If ever a horse was mis-named, it is that one," Stephen said, eyeing the horse with suspicion.

"Well, we cannot all be diamonds of the first water, horse or human," Ella replied. "If you will excuse me, I shall change Beautiful's saddle, your mount is already saddled and waiting."

They rode in silence for some time, the only sound being the horses' hooves along the gravel paths as they made their way to the furthest part of the estate.

"What is that?" Stephen broke the silence, pointing with his riding crop.

"It is part of the building that once stood on this site. There was a priory here, before Henry the Eighth's time," she explained.

"There was a monastery here?"

She shook her head. "A convent, there were never many nuns as far as we know, twelve at most, and many of them were sent by fathers who didn't want to fund a dowry. There were reports of the nuns entertaining gentlemen visitors I believe, so no serious vocations I think."

"Can we get closer?"

"Of course, there is a path, though it may be overgrown now. As far as I know, no-one has been there in some years." She clicked her tongue and Beautiful trotted forwards, but before they had gone far, as she had suspected, the path was overgrown with brambles and bracken, on either side of the path silver birches had grown thick and tall.

"The horses will not like battling their way through the woodland," Ella said. "If we want to go further, we must do it on foot."

After several minutes, Stephen said, "I am beginning to understand the tenacity of the prince in the tale of Sleeping Beauty."

"The brambles are rather thick, I agree, but as far as I recollect, we should be there soon."

No sooner had she replied than the woods and brambles opened out to a grassy area with the ruins of cloisters running around three sides. "I believe the nuns were particularly skilled in copying manuscripts and embroidery, they were not a closed order, so they were able to mix with local people and at the time, did a lot to alleviate the suffering of the poor and sick."

"It seems to have been a harsh life."

She nodded. "Perhaps, but if they came from a poor background, they were probably better clothed, housed and fed than they would have been in the outside world. I believe it was the women who came from more privileged homes who found it difficult to adjust."

"As well they might, particularly if they were dumped here by their fathers."

"I imagine, if my father could have dumped me, he would have done so without a second thought," she replied.

He caught her hand and turned her to face him. "Surely not."

"Oh, I have no doubts on the matter, it would have been the perfect solution for him, no need to fund a dowry and I would have been out of sight and out of mind," she added with a shrug.

He ran his hands up her arms "Listen to me Ella. I do not like to speak ill of your father, but it must be said that he was a cruel, vicious man and a wastrel, all of society knew it, though we did not know quite how cruelly he treated his own daughters. But hear me, you are not only the cleverest woman I have ever met, but the most courageous and lovely one. Any man would and should be proud to have you on his arm."

Ella looked into the depths of his blue eyes. "Thank you, Stephen, that is the nicest thing anyone has ever said to me, and even if only a fraction of it is true, I still thank you. Now," she turned away so that he would not see the tear that had escaped her eye, "what do you know about this potential Tudor monarch?"

He frowned, the damage her father had done was enormous, he wondered if he would ever be able to breach the wall she had erected to protect herself, but what he did know was that, if necessary, he would die trying. "Very little, to be truthful I had never given the idea much consideration until recently when it began to circulate. As I said, the Queen was said to have married Robert Dudley and bore a child both in secret. The child was spirited away and raised, possibly by the Dudleys at one of their estates, or possibly in Wales, or France. Ireland and Scotland are unlikely, given Elizabeth's unpopularity in Ireland and the fact that she had her cousin, Mary, Queen of Scots executed."

"Hmm," she began. "Elizabeth came to the throne in 1558 I believe, now, let us assume that this secret marriage did not take place immediately, she would have needed to consolidate her position as Queen," she mused.

"Go on." Stephen was fascinated to watch as the thoughts crossed her expressive face.

"Let us say that she had the child, say in 1561, and assuming that a generation is roughly thirty-five years, that would mean that we are looking at possibly seven generations of descendants. I wonder that they have not come forward with a claim to the throne before now."

"Do not forget that there were turbulent times after her death, the kings battled with parliament, there was the Civil War and Charles I was beheaded, then there were eleven years of Puritan rule and by the time Charles II came to the throne, the country was grateful for the 'Merry Monarch', the Tudor remnant possibly thought it was not the time. By the time of his mother's death, the child would have been forty, possibly with children of his own and knew that, were he to make a claim to the throne, they would all be thrown into the Tower, a place from which few emerged."

"It does seem improbable," she mused. "And yet..."

"And yet?" he prompted.

"And yet, I can see that there is a romance to this tale that many would love to believe, and who knows? We may, after all, find that there is some truth in it."

Stephen let out a breath. "I hope to God not, I dread to think what this story, if true, will unleash."

CHAPTER 11

They walked on in silence across a patch of grass towards the delicate skeleton of what had once been presumably, a stained-glass window. "I think this was the chapel and beyond the area where the nuns lived," Ella pointed out. "Apparently the nuns physically built the chapel, or the original at any rate."

Stephen's eyebrows raised. "Really?"

"According to a tutor we once had, the original nuns, who may have actually had a vocation, were 'beefy girls' and probably used the five stone method."

"The five stone method?"

"Pile five stones on top of each other, go and have a cup of tea, or more likely ale in those days, and if they are still standing when you come back, add five more."

He threw back his head and laughed. "Not entirely the most technical method but easily tested I suppose."

Ella smiled, it was good to hear him laugh, something she realised she had not heard much and suspected was something of a rarity. "Indeed, though I believe the most recent chapel was built in 1234, by that time, by stonemasons."

"It was destroyed during the reformation I imagine," he suggested.

She shook her head. "The nuns left of course, or rather were thrown out, but the buildings remained. I do not think the priory was really rich enough to be worth Henry bothering with. No, the real damage was done by Oliver Cromwell. Apparently, he, or his men at any rate, used the chapel as a stable and a mortuary after a local battle and when they had no further use for it, they destroyed it. Later, it came into the possession of one of my father's ancestors who used much of the stone to build Swallowfield. As you can see, nothing has disturbed it for many years."

He looked around. "And yet, even after all the violence that happened here, the place has a feeling of peace and tranquillity."

"It is most beautiful in Spring, when the trees are just coming into leaf and the early Spring flowers cover what was once the quadrangle. I think the nuns planted herbs for their medicines, for there is a profusion of wild garlic, rosemary and thyme."

"Did you spend time here as a girl?" he asked.

"It was a useful place to hide when father was in one of his rages."

"Which was?"

She paused. "Often. I have to believe that father loved us in his own way, but the fact is that he had no use for daughters. He saw all of us as a drain on his resources and quite useless as were our mothers for failing to bear him sons and we for not being those sons. His desire for a son drove him, like King Henry, quite mad I think."

He took her hands in his. "Look at me, Ella," he said softly. "Unlike Elliott, I never met your father, so all I know of him are stories that circulated in the ton, but it seems to me that the old Earl had no idea of the diamonds he had, either in his wives or his daughters. The desire for a son to carry on the family line is one all titled families share, but to pursue it to the degree your father did, is unnatural and suggests to me that he suffered from some affliction of the brain. It is perhaps unfair to entirely blame him for the damage that he did, though damage it clearly was."

"Oh, Stephen," was all she could manage.

"I mean it, Ella, you and Verity managed to shield Caro from the worst of his torment, but he was about to marry Verity off to a reprehensible blackguard for his own benefit and as for you," he paused, his finger gently brushing a stray tear from her cheek. "As for you, the worst of his torment was reserved for you because he made you feel that you were not worthy of love because of the scars, which," he held up a hand to stop her from replying, "which are barely visible and that has been the case for years. The greatest damage your father did was how you see yourself. He made you feel small and ugly and that is how you see yourself, but shall I tell you what I see?"

She nodded, mesmerised by the sound of his voice and his eyes which felt as though he could see into her soul. "I see a lovely woman, both outside and in, I see the most beautiful hair, rich and dark with auburn strands which remind me of sunlight catching Autumn leaves and which makes me want to run my hands through it, releasing it from the pins and ribbons so that it falls to your shoulders and beyond, possibly to your waist, but mostly I want to see it on the pillow next to mine. I see your lovely eyes, so expressive, like dark, green pools with tiny flecks of pure gold, they flash like cut emeralds when you are angry, did you know that? Yet now they are pools a man could drown in. I see your lovely nose with its slight upturn which makes me want to kiss it and your generous mouth which I must warn you Ella, I am going to kiss. Now."

He slid his arms around her and pulled her gently towards him as he lowered his head and his lips found hers. "Open for me, Ella," he whispered against her lips and slid his tongue inside, touching, tasting, revelling in the taste of her. One arm went around her waist whilst the other hand gently cupped the back of her head. He wanted to feel as much of her body close to his as possible, he wanted her to feel as much of his body as possible. He could not feel the tips of her nipples harden through the material of their clothing, but if she were even the smallest bit aroused as he was, he knew they would be hard. He almost physically ached to take them in his mouth.

Ella's eyes drifted closed, nothing, nothing in the world mattered more in this moment than the feel of Stephen's lips on hers and his hard, taut body against hers. At some point, and she could not have said when, her arms had gone around his neck and her fingers were caressing the hair at the nape of his neck. His groan as her tongue tentatively touched his, sent her senses flaring, every part of her body was aware of him, the hardness of his thighs and the hardness that pressed into her stomach gave her sensations she had never felt before. She wanted to be touched; she wanted to be touched by Stephen. His words made her feel two things she had never felt, beautiful and desirable.

"I want you, Ella, surely you must know I want you," he whispered, kissing along her jawline. "I want to see you, to hold you, to caress you and taste every part of you." His voice in her ear made her shudder. "Trust me when I say Ella, the scars mean nothing to me." He immediately felt her stiffen and the soft, pliant woman in his arms became rigid. Her hands fell to his chest and she pushed him away. "No Stephen," she said, "this is not right."

"What do you mean?" he asked. "You were made for me Ella, I could feel it."

"No, Stephen, you are mistaken, I was not made for any man. We are working together for the good of the country and that is all. I cannot give you more, I am sorry." She turned and strode past him towards the path.

He watched her retreating figure, her back ramrod straight and tension in every step. Why had he even mentioned the scars? What a fool. He thought he knew how deeply they affected her, but he knew nothing. All he had wanted to do was reassure her and now he had put their budding relationship in jeopardy, though she was still, apparently, prepared to work with him, thank God. She was wrong, she was made for him, they were perfect together, but he would have to think of a new strategy to persuade her. There had been other women since his clumsy proposal years ago, he was not a monk, but none of them meant anything to him. Ella, on the other hand, meant everything.

Back in her room, Ella lay on the bed and looked up at the elaborate canopy. If the scars meant nothing to him, why had he mentioned them? She reached up a hand and gently stroked the slightly ragged skin with her fingertips. Was it the scars or was her reaction due to something else? The fact was, she did not want Stephen to stop, she wanted him to carry on kissing her and she wanted to kiss him back. She wanted to feel his hands on her, she wanted to feel his skin on hers, in short, when he had said he wanted her, the truth was she wanted him as well, and he knew it. Ella hugged her knees, on the one hand, what would it matter if she gave in to her desire for Stephen and let him make love to her and made one wonderful memory to last as she settled into her life as a spinster? She would be ruined of course, but only she and Stephen would know and once they completed this mission, he would no doubt go off once again on a foreign adventure and forget about her. On the other hand, she knew that if she did give herself to him, once he left, her heart would break. What would mean so much to her would probably mean nothing to him. Men, she knew, thought differently about these things.

"Ella, what are you doing?" Verity's voice roused her from her musings as her sister came into the room. "You are supposed to be getting ready for the ball. I have ordered a bath for you and my maid will come and help you dress."

"The ball, I had quite forgotten, I do not feel well Verity, perhaps I should just stay quietly in my room?"

Verity looked at her sister for a moment. "You are rather

flushed, but that is no doubt due to riding out in the cold weather and wandering about the priory ruins with Stephen."

"How did you know?"

Verity laughed. "You know very well, Ella, that no-one can sneeze at Swallowfield without someone finding out. Now stop moping and mooning about Stephen and get ready."

"I am not moping or mooning," Ella protested.

Verity shook her head. "The lady doth protest too much," she quoted. "Stephen is a fine man and would make a wonderful husband. He clearly has feelings for you, but you continually shut him out. He would have married you years ago but for your stubbornness."

"For one thing," Ella counted on her fingers, "Stephen's offer for me made me feel as though I was his last resort and for another, any feelings he has for me are based on lust and nothing more. So once we leave here in a few days, no doubt he will go back to the continent to do whatever it is he does there and I shall go north to visit Aunt Bette's estate near Hawes, she wishes to visit when she comes back from France and would like me to ensure that everything is ready for her arrival. I doubt our paths will cross again."

There was laughter in Verity's eyes. "Definitely protesting too much. However, the debate will have to wait for another day. I shall send Mary to you, and I expect to see you dancing in that lovely new gown." She swept from the room she had, Ella concluded wryly, definitely grown into the role of duchess.

CHAPTER 12

The ball was in full swing when Ella made her entrance. Verity's maid had indeed done a wonder, dressing her hair so that a long curl fell over her shoulder and ensuring that her scars were barely visible. Verity's choice of gown for her was exactly right, the rich gold satin overlaid with a delicate tulle overskirt sprinkled with tiny topaz stones which sparkled as she moved. The high waistline was accented with a deeper topaz sash and the necklace around her throat and the topaz combs in her hair highlighted the golden lights in her eyes. She paused at the top of the stairs to take in the scene before her. Swallowfield had never, in her lifetime, been the venue for a ball, her father had neither the money nor the inclination to host one, but Elliott had restored the house to its former glory and ensured that its ballroom could rival that of any in the county.

One wall had four floor to ceiling windows, leading on to a wide terrace, in case any of the dancers felt the need for some air. The other walls held large mirrors which reflected the many candles in sconces around the walls, candelabra on the side tables and the three chandeliers along the ceiling. The whole effect was of light and colour as the dancers whirled around the room in time, as though worked by clockwork. The chalking on the floor was already beginning to blur as the dancers stepped through the march and were halfway through a quadrille.

"It is a sight to behold," a masculine voice said, close to her ear.

"Indeed," she replied, trying to ignore the shiver down her spine.

"I would be honoured if you would dance the waltz with me," Stephen said.

"I am not sure I shall be dancing this evening," she replied.

"You are looking particularly lovely tonight, Ella. It would be a travesty not to allow the young men of the county the opportunity to dance with you."

She turned to him. "Why are you doing this Stephen?"

"Doing what?" he asked, innocently.

"You know perfectly well what. Flirting, complimenting and kissing me, and pretending that there is something between us when we both know there is not."

"Ah but there is Ella, yet you seem determined to deny it," he responded. "However, we made an agreement to be friends and that is what I intend to be, if we are to work together we have to be able to trust each other, and it will be easier if we are able to at least try to get along." He held out his hand. "Come, the waltz is about to begin."

"I thought you might like to know," he said as he took her in his arms and drew her close, "that my man of business forwarded my correspondence and, as we theorised, I have an invitation to a masquerade at Bolton Castle on Valentine's Day."

"Oh, my goodness, then we were right." Ella could scarcely breathe.

"You were right, Ella, you were the one to decipher the code," he replied. “I now have a way into the event, but we must plan to ensure that the conspirators are captured.”

“I will consider how I will be able to gain entry,” she mused.

“Ella, there is no need for you to be involved in the actual event, I shall gather together loyal men, and we will ensure that the conspirators are caught and brought to justice.”

Ella’s eyes flashed liquid gold at him. “Do you not remember discussing this very issue with you Stephen? At the moment we do not even know who is loyal and who is not. As to the matter of the event at Bolton Castle, you gave your word, which as a gentleman, I expect you to honour.”

He shook his head, lifting an eyebrow at her. “Now I am inwardly rolling my eyes. One way or the other, you, Lady Ella, are likely to be the death of me. Now, the question is, how are we to get you to Bolton Castle? I have a small estate not far from Wensley which I can use as a base, it is near enough to the castle but far enough away from prying eyes.”

She curtseyed as the final strains of the waltz died away. “I shall give the matter some thought, ask me for the supper dance and we can discuss the matter further,” she said, boldly.

His eyebrows rose. “Two dances, Ella? There will be talk, but I should be honoured if you would keep the supper dance for me.” He bowed and escorted her to where Verity was standing before striding off in the direction of the library.

“Aha,” Verity said, with a gleam in her eye. “So it seems that I was right concerning Stephen.”

“I have no idea what you are talking about,” Ella replied.

“Of course you do,” Verity scoffed. “There is something between Stephen and you, there always has been and, if you had not been so stubborn years ago, you would be married and the

Duchess of Hart with a brood of little Harts running around by now."

"You have clearly been reading too many of those romantic novels you are so addicted to."

"I know what I know," Verity replied, with a grin.

"And what you do not know, it seems you are entirely comfortable with making up," Ella said with more conviction than she felt.

Until the supper waltz, Ella was content to stand at the side of the room and watch the dancers, she was quite used to not attracting attention to herself and had positioned herself between a large potted palm and one of the marble columns when she heard an unfamiliar voice.

"All the invitations have been dispatched. We need men of real influence to put their voices and money behind the cause. My bet is that Hart will become part of the brotherhood, he has been out of the country for many years, such is his distaste for the current rulers."

"Indeed? I heard he intends to return and has been squiring the sister of the duchess around, the ugly one with the scars. The one he danced with earlier."

"I did not notice the scars, but no matter, ugly or not, it matters little when the candles are snuffed out."

"Of course, no doubt she is grateful for anyone to bed her for no man will want to wed her."

"It is not her face he will be looking at when she opens her legs for him."

Both men laughed as they walked away, Ella craned her neck but all she could get was a glimpse of their backs, one in a puce satin tailcoat, the other in a gold brocade. She would not be able to recognise their faces, but she would remember their clothing, and she would never forget their words.

It seemed no time at all before Stephen was standing in front of her. "My dance I believe, Lady Ella." He frowned. "Are you all right Ella, you are very pale."

"I am fine," she replied.

"Then why is your hand trembling in mine?" He grazed his thumb across her palm.

"It is of no matter," she said as they made their way onto the floor. "Do you see the two gentlemen over there by the entrance to the terrace, the ones in puce and gold brocade, but when you look, try not to make it obvious."

"Lord Henry Clapham and the Earl of Fulwood, both distant acquaintances of Elliot's but were in the area when the invitations to the ball went out, guests of Lord Upton I believe. Why?"

Ella looked around her before leaning in, "I will tell you during supper, what I have to say cannot be overheard."

"In which case," he drew her closer, "let us at least pretend to enjoy this waltz, giving anyone who notices that we are carefree." He smiled down at her and gave her hand a gentle squeeze. "And during supper you will also tell me what upset you."

Ella eyed the plate of food that Stephen placed in front of her, chicken and ham, glazed carrots and poached salmon as well as pies and several kinds of cheese. "Thank goodness you did not bring white soup, I cannot abide it," she murmured, "but I shall not be able to eat all of this."

"Nonsense, you eat barely enough to keep a sparrow alive, and," he added leaning scandalously close. "The longer we take to eat, the longer we shall have time to talk."

"Very well." Ella picked up her knife and fork. "To keep up the appearance that we are talking of trivialities, we should laugh from time to time."

Stephen let out a genuine burst of laughter. "And to think I was working with a rank amateur. I think Sir Robert would be only too happy to sign you up as an agent in your own right. Now," he lowered his voice, "tell me of your interest in Clapham and Fulwood."

"I overheard them whilst I was watching the dancing. I do not know who said what because I could not see, but they are, I am sure conspirators, they knew you had received an invitation to Bolton Castle, they believe you to be disenchanted with the governance of the country and see you as a potential conspirator. They believe that a man of your power and influence will greatly add weight to their campaign."

"Good God," Stephen exclaimed. "These are men I have exchanged greetings with at social gatherings, but that is, as far as I am aware, all. I believe Clapham is all but bankrupt, his family's finances were decimated when the South Sea Bubble burst and none of his ancestors has had the wit or work ethic to restore them. Fulwood has ample funds since his marriage to an heiress, the daughter of a steel maker from Sheffield apparently. The father wanted a title for his daughter and Fulwood wanted the money, I do not think the match is a happy one."

Ella dropped her fan so that Stephen could pick it up and present it to her with a teasing smile. "For someone who claims not to know them, you seem to know quite a bit about them," she commented, taking the fan and opening it.

He smiled and offered her a glass of ratafia. "There are few secrets in the ton regarding money and marriage."

She shook her head, "No thank you, ratafia is far too sweet, in fact all the drinks offered to women are far too sweet, but that is an argument for another day." She waved her fan slowly, a great sign to anyone watching that they were in the middle of a flirtation.

"So what was it that upset you, Ella?" Stephen asked. "Because knowing you as I do, you were not fazed at all by the discovery of conspirators in our midst."

"They made some derogatory remarks about one of your dance partners," she replied.

"But I have only danced with you," he paused as realisation dawned. "What did they say?"

"It is of no consequence, but I have had an idea about how I might gain entry to the Valentines Ball."

CHAPTER 13

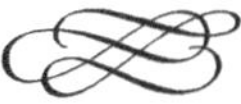

"Absolutely not," he exclaimed. "On no account, Ella, and that is final. It is beyond me that you could even consider such a thing appropriate."

"But it is the perfect way, no-one notices servants, no-one will know who I am and a servant can often eavesdrop without their master or mistress suspecting. You and I both know that the servants in a household know all its secrets well before their employers, and possibly the secrets of other houses as well, given the efficiency of the servant grapevine," she replied, calmly.

"All of that may be true, but what if you are found out? These men will stop at nothing to achieve their aim, and I cannot risk you being harmed."

"Then how did you imagine I might be of help when you gave me your word that I could accompany you?" she demanded.

"In all honesty I promised you that you could come in the hope of persuading you otherwise before the event, I had quite underestimated how stubborn you are," he said with a heavy sigh. "But I thought you might stay safe at my estate and decipher any further document that might fall in our hands. I did not envisage you taking part in any of the action and putting your life in danger," he admitted.

Ella could have given him a shake. "That is just typical of the male mind, I am not at all stubborn, it is just that you do not think women can be relied upon or trusted to accomplish anything of use or purpose. So let me be clear, duke, if you do not take me with you to Yorkshire, I shall find a way to get there by myself."

"And if that is not the very definition of stubborn, I do not know what is," he responded. "Very well, I see that you are not to be denied, but you must promise that you will obey orders like a good soldier. I cannot risk having to rescue you or being distracted from the mission by your presence."

"For one thing," she tapped him lightly on the arm with her fan, "you will not need to rescue me and for another I have no intention of distracting you from the mission and finally, when the orders are sound, I shall have no difficulty in obeying them."

"Hmm, the latter I very much doubt," he said. Part of him was terrified that he was putting Ella in harm's way, but another part of him knew that she desperately wanted to be of service, to prove something to herself and others, that women mattered, that she mattered, and a further part admitted that he wanted to keep her close to him at all times.

"Very well. We will consider a plan to travel north as soon as possible in order to make the necessary preparations." He held out his hand. Ella held out hers and he took it, but instead of shaking it as she expected, he turned it over and planted a kiss on her wrist. "There, the bargain is temporarily sealed with a kiss." He raised his head and looked into her eyes, seeing the flash of attraction she was not quick enough to hide.

"What do you mean, temporarily?" Her voice was husky.

"I think an agreement as serious as the one we have just made requires more than a paltry kiss on the wrist, but we shall keep it for when we are more private." His voice was low with sensual promise.

"I have not agreed to kiss you," she protested, weakly.

"Oh, you will, my dear," he replied. "You have inveigled yourself into this mission, but everything comes at a price my lady and this is my price."

"Oh, very well, one kiss."

"One kiss," he agreed. For now.

The rest of the ball passed in a whirl, as Ella had already danced, she was bound by etiquette to dance with any gentleman who asked, though, as usual only a few of the older gentlemen asked. The younger ones preferred to dance with the young debutantes at which Ella was neither surprised nor upset, she had spent the few balls she had been permitted to attend watching as Verity danced. What she had honed in that time was her talent for observation which would no doubt come in useful in what lay ahead. As she lay in bed her thoughts turned to Stephen and his demand for a kiss, she shivered at the thought. Stephen was getting close, too close, dangerously close and if she was to survive the next few weeks she had to find the determination to stay a step away from him.

The question of how to travel to Yorkshire without arousing suspicion was thankfully solved by Aunt Bette who sent a letter informing Ella that her sojourn in the south of France had done her the world of good and that she wished to travel to the Yorkshire estate in the Spring and would Ella travel ahead and ensure that the preparations for opening up the house were in place for her arrival.

"How fortuitous," Stephen drawled as Ella read out the letter. "When I leave here, I intend to go to the Wensley estate, perhaps I might escort you. It would be safer than travelling alone."

"How kind," she replied, with a wink.

"That is a wonderful idea." Verity looked up from her embroidery. "I shall feel much better knowing that Ella is not travelling by post-chase alone."

"It will be my pleasure," Stephen said with a smile.

"How fortuitous that your aunt wishes to visit Yorkshire," Stephen commented quietly when they were enjoying a game of chess after dinner.

"Indeed," Ella replied, moving her knight and taking his remaining bishop.

"And so convenient as regards timing." He moved his queen to a safer space.

"I agree." She studied the board for a moment before moving her bishop and declaring, "Checkmate."

"What?" Stephen looked at the board in surprise.

"Your king is in check by my bishop, and should you remove it with your queen I shall take her with my rook and put the king in check again," she explained.

"A resounding win, I congratulate you." His smile indeed reached his eyes.

"It always pays to have a sound strategy." She smiled back as she replaced the pieces in the box.

"Why do I have the impression that your last comment was not, in fact, related to our game of chess?"

"I have no idea," she replied, "but we should perhaps consider what we might find at Bolton Castle and prepare several plans."

"We shall discuss it when we reach Wensley and have a better idea of what we are facing," he confirmed.

Ella nodded, it was the first time that Stephen had spoken to her as though she was an equal and indeed part of the plan.

The journey to Yorkshire would take the best part of five days, the weather had turned since Christmas, snow had fallen in the north and as far south as Derbyshire according to the vicar, whose sister lived near Bakewell.

"I think it best if you travel as my sister," Stephen said as he handed her into his carriage, "that way, no eyebrows will be raised at the prospect of a young lady travelling alone with a gentleman. I discussed the matter with both Elliott and Verity, and they are of the opinion that it is the best way of not attracting attention to us and avoiding scandal."

"You might have discussed it with me," she huffed. "But I concur, a single lady travelling would probably attract a great deal of attention and that is what we must avoid."

"At last, the lady agrees with me," he said with a flourish.

"Only out of necessity," she said, firmly.

"So when does your aunt intend to arrive in Yorkshire?"

"Never I imagine, she is quite enjoying her time in the south of France and has found Yorkshire too cold, especially in winter, for years."

He raised his eyebrows. "But you said she wanted you to open up the house for her," he spluttered.

"Indeed, I did," she replied, calmly.

"You said you had a letter from her."

"I did, it is just that the letter I received did not mention going to Yorkshire," she explained.

"So you lied?"

"I did." She shrugged. "Had I not, I rather fancy that you would have found some excuse to avoid keeping your promise for me to be involved. So I consider that we are equal in that regard. Am I correct?" She waited for his response before adding, "I shall take your silence on the matter as an admission that that was exactly what you planned to do."

"It was for your own good," he ground out.

"In future, I will thank you to allow me to determine what is or is not for my own good."

Stephen was silent for a moment. "Would I be correct in assuming that this is an example of how ladies' lives are restricted?" he asked.

She nodded.

"Then I shall endeavour to ask in future, rather than assume," he stated.

"Thank you," she replied, smiling.

At that moment, Stephen realised he would do anything to have Ella smile at him, a genuine smile, from the heart. He wanted this woman with every fibre of his being, not just her body, though heaven knew he craved that, but he wanted to wake up with her in the morning, spend time talking with her, listening to her views, debating with her, challenging her as she would challenge him. He wanted to make her laugh and know that she was both loved and cherished, and, if for some reason she was crying, he wanted to be the one to take her in his arms and comfort her. Her father had done his best to break her spirit, but she had refused to be broken, he was in awe of her strength and the thought of someone taking her away from him filled him with dread.

"I will do everything in my power to ensure that you are fully included in future discussions and planning in this mission," he said, finally. "But I cannot promise that, should you come to be in harm's way I shall not take immediate action to ensure you are safe. I cannot bear the thought of you being injured or worse, not because of Elliott or Verity, but because of my feelings toward you." He held up a hand, "It is not because I see you as a weak woman, because I do not, it is not because I feel pity for you on account of the scars, I do not, you have prevailed because you are one of the strongest people I know, man or woman. It is because I personally could not bear it if harm should come to you, I shall say no more for the moment Ella, but soon we shall have an honest conversation about us. Can you live with that?"

CHAPTER 14

Ella was grateful for once that she did not have to reply as the carriage was pulling into the yard of The Bear in Oxford, where they were to spend the night. Stephen's words had shocked her, for so long she had lived her life without the hope or expectation that anyone, other than her sisters knew who she really was. All they ever saw was what was on the outside and usually that was enough for them to dismiss her as unworthy of their attention, let alone respect. And yet, Stephen could not bear it if harm should come to her? Did that mean he cared? Dare she even think there might be something more? She quickly banished the thought, a happy ever after was not for her. She was too old, too cynical, too damaged for it to mean anything more than the friendship he had already offered. Once this adventure was over, he would go back to his exciting life wherever it took him, he would marry a debutante and produce the requisite heir and she would go back to her quiet life as a spinster, and that was that. Yet, as he handed her down from the carriage, she felt a shiver go through her body as he held her hand.

"I sent ahead and ensured that we have good rooms and a

decent dinner," Stephen said, as they walked towards the door. "How do you feel like taking a stroll before we dine? After a day enclosed in a carriage, my bones would welcome a chance to unwind."

"I think that is an excellent idea," she replied.

"I must confess, I have always been curious about the city," Ella said, as they walked down the High Street. "It is so beautiful with magnificent buildings."

"Indeed, it is," Stephen replied. "Though in all honesty, the taverns are likely to get somewhat unruly when the students are in residence."

"Are you speaking from experience?" She smiled up at him.

He laughed. "Well, I cannot say that I visited all of them, there being about four hundred I believe, but I did my best to ensure that as many tavern keepers as possible had a decent income."

When they reached the Radcliffe Camera, Ella sighed. "It must have been wonderful to have been a student here."

Stephen thought for a moment. "It was, though I suspect, like most of the young men here, I did not fully appreciate it at the time."

"Perhaps there will come a time when women are able to study here," she mused.

"Perhaps," he agreed, "though I doubt that the learned, ancient dons I studied under would have the first idea how to deal with a room full of young ladies asking questions. As it happens, they are not allowed to marry, so their contact with women other than their mothers and sisters has been limited, they would be more afraid of any young ladies than the young ladies would be of them."

Ella thought that quite funny. "I have a picture of an elderly white-haired gentleman standing on a chair in the corner, while a pack of young ladies surround him, brandishing books."

"That is probably exactly what would happen'." He joined in

her laughter. "Come, we should return to The Bear, our dinner awaits.

"The Bear is known for its excellent food," Stephen said, spearing a slice of roast beef.

"So I see," Ella replied.

"Any yet you have barely touched a thing."

Ella placed her cutlery together. "The food is delicious, but I find I am too tired to enjoy it. If you do not mind, I shall retire to my room."

Stephen stood. "Of course, I hope you do not mind, but I arranged for you to have a bath. I thought you might appreciate the chance to wash away the dirt of the day. Travelling is always a grimy business."

"Thank you," she replied. "That is most kind."

"I shall follow you up, we leave at first light tomorrow, so an early night will benefit us both." As soon as the words were out of his mouth, he almost groaned at the thought of Ella lying in the bed in the room next to his. Just the thought of her hair spread out on the pillow was enough for his body to harden. Yet she had no idea of the effect she had on him.

Twenty minutes later, Ella gave up the struggle, no matter how she twisted her body this way and that, she could not reach the laces at the back of her bodice. The copper bathtub was steaming invitingly, but unless she could get out of her gown, the water would go cold and the effort of bringing up to her room and filling it would be wasted. There was nothing for it, she would have to ask for help. Stephen opened the door almost as soon as she knocked on it. He had removed his coat, neckcloth and waistcoat and stood before her in his white shirt, the sleeves rolled up to reveal his sinuous forearms, his shirt was undone and she could clearly see the outline of his muscles and sprinkling of chest hair, which narrowed as it disappeared into his trousers.

"Ella, what are you doing? You know you should not be anywhere near my room, especially not alone."

"Then you need to come to mine," she said, turning and walking down the corridor."

"Close the door," she said as he followed her into the room.

"Are you deliberately trying to ruin yourself?" he demanded.

"Not at all, you preposterous man, I simply need you to help with the laces on my gown. Unfortunately, I do not have a maid with me, as you know, the fewer people who know about where we are going and why, precluded additional servants."

His eyebrows rose. "You want me to undress you?"

She rolled her eyes. "The laces on my gown tie at the back, I have tried to unfasten them, but they seem to be in a bit of a muddle, if you would be so good as to unlace me, I can make use of the bath you so thoughtfully ordered for me. Preferably before it goes cold."

"Turn around," he ordered.

Ella's breath hitched as she saw them in the cheval mirror, he was standing so close she could feel his breath on her neck as he worked the laces free and slid the bodice from her shoulders. She almost stopped breathing altogether when his hands went to the laces on her skirt. Within moments, her skirt and petticoats lay in a pool at her feet, and she stood before him in only her stockings and thin chemise.

She caught sight of Stephen's eyes reflected in the glass. "I should go," he murmured, "but I find I cannot. The only thing I want to do, need to do, is to kiss you." He watched as her eyes darkened and noticed her almost imperceptible nod, he almost cheered, for it seemed that as much as he wanted to kiss her, she wanted him too. He lifted her hair from her shoulder, gently pushed her chemise aside and kissed her from her neck to her shoulder before turning her around and pulling her towards him, one arm went around her waist and the other cupped the back of her head as he lowered his lips to hers.

As soon as his lips touched hers Ella felt as though her whole body had been swept up in a restless tide of desire, her body felt boneless, as though she would fall were it not for Stephen's strong arms holding her. When he touched his tongue to her lips, she instinctively opened for him and could not help a small shudder as his tongue touched hers. Her hands gripped the front of his shirt, he hissed a breath as her fingers came into contact with his bare skin. His hand slipped to her bottom and eased her closer, every part of her body felt alive to his touch.

He could feel her shudder as he outlined the shell of her ear with the tip of his tongue. "I swear Ella, there is no other woman in the world who can do this to me," he whispered, pressing his hard length against her soft curves.

"Stephen...I..." her tone of voice broke through the erotic web he was wove and he realised she was shaking.

"Ella, are you all right?" He paused, looking once again into the deep pools of her eyes. "Are you afraid of me?" he asked. "You know I would never do anything to harm you."

She shook her head and took a step back. "I know, and I am not afraid of you, but I am afraid of ...this." She threw her arm out in a gesture. "I am afraid of where this will lead. When life returns to normal, because we both know that what we are about to embark on is anything but normal."

"You believe that these feelings we both have for each other." He held up a hand as she was about to speak. "Please do not try to deny it Ella, you have feelings for me, I see it in your eyes, and I felt it when you were in my arms. You believe these feelings, "he continued, "are heightened because we are about to embark on a mission which is dangerous and from which one or both of us might not emerge. Is that it?"

Ella nodded, "In essence, yes."

He rested his forehead against hers, before stepping back, raising his head and kissing the tip of her nose, "May God preserve me from a woman who is clearly more intelligent than I. In some respects, I believe you may be right, danger does make people behave in ways they would normally eschew, everything seems to be heightened, colours are brighter, sounds more intense and so it seems perhaps are feelings. But I would say this Ella, when this is over, assuming that we both survive, you and I will have a conversation about our future relationship. For I do not believe the feelings I have for you can be explained as a result of the mission we are about to undertake. I will say no more for the present. Now, enjoy your bath." He stepped away and left the room without looking back.

Ella stood looking at the door as though it could give her an answer. What did he mean, his feelings for her? And there was no point in denying it, she had feelings for him, feelings she had tried to bury but it was no good, she was in love with him, had always been in love with him and would always be in love with him. But was it possible that he loved her? He respected her, that she knew and when they were not arguing, seemed to regard her with some sort of brotherly affection, but could it really be more than that? She shook her head, no, it was not possible, they were about to face a difficult foe and what he felt for her was lust, she had heard that men needed to slake their desires before battles, that was why there were many women of low repute who followed armies around as camp followers, receiving payment for their services. Well, she would stand firm, regardless of Stephen's fine words, she would always be the one who loved and, in the end, she knew in her heart that she would never be enough for him. The time would come when he would break her heart and that she could not allow.

I will stay strong, I must stay strong, she repeated to herself as she stepped into her now tepid bath.

CHAPTER 15

"I trust you slept well," Stephen said as he boarded the carriage. It had nearly killed him to walk away from her the night before, he had longed to strip the last layer of thin fabric from her body and feast his eyes on her nakedness, to see her nipples harden as he looked at her and to feel the weight of her breasts in his hands as he caressed them. Even now, just the thought of her made him harden and he took his seat quickly.

"Tolerably well, thank you," she lied. Ella had tossed and turned all night unable to stop the flow of thoughts and feelings fizzing through her as she wondered what would have happened had she not stopped Stephen when she did. Would it be wrong to let him make love to her? Under normal circumstances the very thought would almost have been enough to ruin her, but they were living in anything other than normal circumstances. She did not want to die without experiencing a man's touch and if she did not return from this mission, who would know that she did not die an innocent? And if she did return back to her life as a spinster, at least she would have a memory of what it was to have been loved, or lusted after at least.

"Do you agree?"

Ella was suddenly conscious that Stephen had been talking. "I apologise, I was wool gathering, please, what did you say?"

"I was suggesting that we explain your presence to my staff that you were en-route to your aunt's house but received word that there was some problem with the building, a chimney fell down or some such and you will be staying with me until the work has been completed."

"Oh, that will not be necessary," she replied. "My aunt's old housekeeper retired to a small cottage in Castle Bolton where she grew up, Castle Bolton is the village that surrounds the castle. I have arranged to stay with her and shall seek employment at the castle, the event they are planning will mean that they will need to take on more servants. What could be more convenient than living at the foot of the castle?"

"The hell you will," Stephen roared. "We have already discussed this, and I will not allow you to put yourself in a situation where I cannot guarantee your safety."

She turned to him. "Stephen, we both know that you cannot guarantee either my safety or yours. How else can I get into the castle to find out information? I am not invited to the ball and in any case, there will be times during the preparations that things may be discussed that might be of use to us."

"I could always put one or two of my men in as servants."

"That would be a good idea, but in my experience, gentlemen will often speak more freely in front of a woman, especially a servant because they do not believe we have the wit to understand what they are talking about," she replied.

"I just do not like the idea that I will be unable to protect you," he admitted to her and to himself. The thought that she would be at the castle when he was not there filled him with dread.

She took his hands in hers and looked at him for the first time since they entered the carriage. "Stephen, even in normal life it is not possible to protect someone all the time, people have accidents, people get sick, we just have to do our best. But I promise I shall not take any unnecessary risks, does that make you feel easier?"

He nodded, though in his heart he did not. "How do you propose to pass yourself off convincingly as a servant?" he asked.

"Firstly, I shall ask Mrs. Gamble, Aunt Bette's old house-keeper, if she knows of any work going at the castle, and present myself there. If they want a cook, scullery maid, lady's maid, whatever they want, that is what I shall claim to be."

"And how will you do that? Have you experience in any of this work? Having a lady's maid is not the same as being one and as for cooking and washing pots and pans? Your hands alone tell that you are not used to work of that kind," he pointed out.

She took a deep breath. "I do not think you are fully aware of the situation in which we were living before Verity and your brother were forced to marry. Father had died leaving us nothing but debt, but even before he died there was little money, he had to let most of the servants go because he could not afford to pay them. Verity and I learned both to cook and clean because there was no-one else to do it. I admit that work as a scullery maid does not particularly appeal to me and I should imagine that also goes for those who from accident of birth are forced to do such work, but if that is what needs to be done, that is what I shall do."

"I cannot say I am happy about this, Ella, but I do see the sense of it," he admitted. "However, I shall ensure that there are several of my men sent as servants to the castle, as you say the event is a large one and many servants will be needed and who knows what information might be gleaned from loose talk."

"Exactly."

He sat back and stared out of the window, though noticed little of the countryside, his thoughts were consumed by the woman sitting across from him. Not only was she prepared to undertake serious physical risks, but she was also proving herself to be quite an astute strategist. Though, had he the option of sending a female agent into the castle he would have forbidden Ella from setting foot in the place. He grinned to himself, the thought of forbidding Ella to do anything and her obeying was laughable, she was a woman of spirit, something he had not fully appreciated until now. In fact, there were many things he had not appreciated, her wit, her liveliness, her courage and her intellect, not to mention the fact that behind the cool exterior she presented to the world, there was a passionate woman, one he intended would be his one day, and the sooner the better. He had wasted too many years without her, and he had no intention of wasting more. He just had to work out how to breach the wall she had built around herself. It would require a great deal of patience and persistence, the persistence he could manage, but the patience was quite another matter.

As the carriage rumbled on to their next destination, Ella sat with a book on her lap, occasionally stealing a glance at Stephen, though he seemed to be absorbed in his own thoughts and almost unaware of her presence. She had dreaded the thought of seeing him over the festive season and now she was embarking on an exciting and potentially dangerous quest with him. The thought of what they were about to do was both exhilarating and terrifying, yet she knew that Stephen trusted her and had come, although grudgingly at times, to respect her ideas and opinions. Whether his feelings ran any deeper, she had yet to find out.

When they stopped briefly for a bite to eat and to stretch their legs, it was noticeable that the weather had gone colder, a bitter wind blew from the east and there were traces of snow on the ground. Ella saw little of Stephen as his travelling desk was unpacked and he spent much of the time writing letters to be taken by the next mail coach. As they set off once again, Ella was grateful for the heated brick he had had placed in the carriage and the extra blanket, it seemed that for each mile they travelled the temperature dropped.

When they stopped at Stilton, a few flakes of snow were falling. "I thought we would make fewer stops," Ella said as she took Stephen's hand down from the coach.

"As the weather is unpredictable at this time of year and the days are at their shortest, I thought it best to take more time and ensure that we arrived each night at an inn, I have travelled too many times when I have had to sleep in a cold coach, and to be honest, it is not something I recommend. I also," he added with a grin, "wanted to make sure that we got a good dinner."

She gave him a wry look. "Trust you to think of your creature comforts."

His eyes darkened as he recalled sleeping in barns if he was lucky, but sometimes hedgerows and ditches and one time he had to spend many hours underneath the bodies of fallen comrades as the enemy searched for battle survivors.

"What?" Ella asked. "What did I say to cause such a countenance?"

"Nothing." He forced a smile; there were parts of his life that no-one needed to know about. "The inn is called The Bell, and you will appreciate the cheese here, the local farmers make it and sell it to travellers. Its flavour is quite unique."

"Why do I get the feeling that you are changing the subject?" she said as they entered the warmth of the inn.

"You were quite right," she admitted at the end of the meal. "The cheese was delicious, as was the rest of the meal." She yawned.

"For some reason, travel seems to make me tired, even though I have done no activity other than read for two days."

"We shall make an early start tomorrow, our next stop is further, and the weather is closing in. I shall come to your room in a few minutes to assist you with your clothing." His voice was clipped, the thought of undressing Ella each night brought both feelings of delight and dread. The more he was forced to help Ella, the more he wanted to remove every last stitch of her clothing and feast his eyes, before using his hands and mouth to give her as much pleasure as he could. He could, of course, have asked the landlord's wife or daughter to assist Ella, but he had not because he treasured those intimate moments, or he was a complete blackguard who was taking advantage of the situation Ella found herself in?

When he entered the room, Ella was standing in front of the cheval mirror, struggling with her hands behind her back. "I managed to tie the laces this morning, but now they are in a tangle," she explained. "Then please allow me." He turned and locked the door before standing behind her. "This could take some time," he said as he began to untie the knots.

All Ella could do was look at Stephen through the mirror, his dark hair flopped over his forehead as he bent towards her, he was handsome, she could not deny it. His eyes were hidden beneath the lush, dark lashes any woman would have been proud of, his nose was straight and his lips parted slightly as he concentrated. She already knew how it would feel to have those lips touch her own. But how would it feel to have those strong hands on her body?

"There," he said, stepping back slightly and easing the bodice from her shoulders, "you are free." He cleared his throat. "Do you need assistance with your skirts, or can you manage?"

"I believe some assistance would be welcome," she replied, her voice low. "When they lay in a pool at her feet, he turned to go.

"Wait," she said. "Wait, please. I do not want you to go."

He turned. "Yes, you do, or you should, because if I stay everything will change."

CHAPTER 16

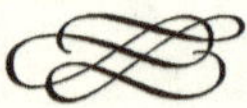

"Then let it change," she said, her hands swiftly dispensing with the ties on her petticoat as it drifted down to join her other clothes on the floor.

"Ella, what are you doing?" His voice was hoarse.

"I am taking control of my destiny," she replied, reaching for ties on her stays. "As you have pointed out to me on several occasions now, we are about to embark on a mission from which one or both of us may not return, but if I am to be the one, I do not want to leave this life without knowing what it is to have a man make love to me."

"This is wrong, Ella," he desperately tried to reason, though his cock was already aching with need.

Her hands stilled. "Fine, if you do not want me, I shall find someone who does. Someone who is not disgusted by my scars."

He strode towards her. "The hell you will."

The corset fell to the floor. "Why should I not? If you do not want me..."

He ran a hand through his hair. "If I do not want you? I have wanted you for years, Ella. You haunt my dreams when I am asleep and my thoughts when I am awake. I want you with every fibre of my being, have no doubt about that."

She paused. "I sense a but coming."

"For God's sake, Ella, you are my sister-in-law. If I were to ruin you my own brother would probably call me out." She was now clad only in the flimsiest of chemises, he could not take his eyes from her, the fabric was so fine he could see the dark outline of her nipples and a dark triangle over her womanhood."

Realisation dawned. "What did you say about your scars?" The chemise inched higher.

"That I would find someone who was not disgusted by my scars."

With a swift movement, she was in his arms, and his lips were crushed against his, one hand tangled in her hair and the other held her close, moulding her softness to his hard body. He ran his tongue along her lips and she opened for him, making him growl as her tongue delicately touched his. He loosened his hold and took a slight step back. "Is this what you really want?" he asked. "Because if you want to stop this, now is the time."

He almost groaned in disappointment when she stepped back from him, but if that is what she had decided, then he would abide by her wishes, even if it killed him. His eyes opened wide when she bent to grasp the hem of her chemise and wrenched it over her head, standing before him clad only in her stockings held up by rose coloured garters. It was the most erotic sight he had seen.

"My God, Ella, you are perfect," he breathed as his eyes roamed her naked body, her pert, full breasts, her narrow waist and flat stomach and lower to the neat dusting of hair covering her womanhood.

"Not perfect," she contradicted, pushing the heavy weight of her hair from her shoulder. "It is as well that you look at this now," she said, quietly.

The scars ran from her ear, down her neck, shoulder and down the top of her arm. The skin was shiny and puckered and slightly lighter than the skin elsewhere on her body, but the scars were almost faded. "This is who I am, Stephen," she went on. "My father called me damaged and worthless. He could barely look at me, especially when I was a child. He said that no man would want to bed me, even in the dark."

"Your father, God rot his soul, was the biggest fool in the country. He could not see goodness and real beauty if it bit him on the arse. You are quite lovely, Ella, and you are intelligent, wise, kind and good. You have scars through no fault of your own, but they have been in part, the making of you. So I would say, I have seen them and I am not disgusted by them, far from it. They are one small part of you and in many ways they make me admire you more."

"Thank you," she said softly.

He stepped towards her and gently pulled her into his arms. "All I want in this moment is to kiss you, to touch you, to taste you, Ella."

"Then what are you waiting for?" she asked.

"I want to know that this is also what you want," he explained.

"I have already said so."

"Then God help me, I cannot refuse," he murmured as he kissed behind her ear and down her jawline, dropping kisses the entire length of her scar before turning his attention to her mouth. As soon as his lips touched hers, it was as though a bolt of lightning coursed through her entire body, his arms went around her, pressing her to him. They were both breathless when he raised his head. "Come," he said, taking her hand and leading her to the bed. "Let me worship and pleasure you, lovely Ella." He drew back to covers and eased her onto the soft mattress before kneeling and unfastening her garters and slowly sliding her stockings from her legs. When she lay before him, he gazed at her body before running a finger from her throat to her nipple watching it harden at his touch before he bent his head and kissed it. He smiled as he felt a shiver run through her body, "You like that?" he enquired.

"Yes," was all she could manage.

He turned his attention to the other nipple, replacing his lips with his fingers as he stroked and caressed her breast. "Oh," she sighed, her whole body felt restless and she could not help but move against his hand, and when one slid towards her most intimate place she drew in a sharp breath.

"Stop squirming, Ella." She could hear the amusement in his voice.

"I cannot help it, I have never...oh." She gasped as his fingers parted and slid inside her.

"Dear God, you are so wet and ready for me," he murmured as he began to move his fingers.

"Is that normal? Because I have never done this before and I am not sure of what I should do," she said, with an honesty that touched his heart.

"On this occasion, sweet Ella, you need do nothing, this time it is all about your pleasure. There will be other times when we shall do things that require, shall we say, a little more energy on your part than today, but tonight is for you, so relax and let me take care of you."

"But..." she began.

"No buts, or I shall have to take off my neckcloth and gag you," he interrupted, with a wicked gleam in his eye. "Though the prospect of you bound and gagged so that I may have you helpless in order to pleasure you for hours does have its attractions."

Ella's eyes were wide, but she said nothing. His head dipped further and he nudged her legs wider so that he could settle himself between her thighs. When he withdrew his finger and kissed her mound, she almost shot off the bed. He licked her entrance before plunging his tongue inside her soft folds, finding the small nub he knew would give her the most intense pleasure. It was not long before Ella was restlessly moving against him, soft mewing sounds came from her throat that she didn't even realise she was making. He watched her face as he inserted two fingers inside her and began to stroke again, his thumb concentrating on the small nub, "That's it, Ella, come for me, reach for it my sweet and I shall give it to you." His voice was quiet as he watched the emotions play across her expressive face.

"Oh, my goodness, Stephen, I can't...Oh," she gasped, her entire body shaking with tremors.

When, eventually she stilled, she looked at him. "I never realised anything could feel like that."

"Of course not, you are an innocent, technically at any rate." He smiled.

"It does not seem at all fair," she replied.

He raised his eyebrows, was Ella regretting what they had just done? "Fair?"

"Well, innocent or not, I most certainly experienced pleasure, but what of you? It does not seem in the slightest fair that, for example, you are fully dressed, whilst I am not wearing a stitch of clothing."

He threw back his head and laughed. "Ella, you are going to be the death of me. It is true that when we fully consummate our relationship, I fully intend that neither of us should be wearing a stitch of clothing, though the fact that you are naked and I am fully clothed is actually quite arousing. As to my pleasure, I shall take care of myself when I return to my room."

"But can I not do something to alleviate your...?" Her eyes darted to the bulge in his trousers.

He raised his eyes to heaven and took a breath before replying, "No Ella, not tonight. If I were less than a gentleman I would happily take everything you offer and believe me that is exactly what I want to do, but I will not take your virginity, we both know that what we are about to embark on is going to be difficult and dangerous. It may be that I do not survive and, that being the case, I should like to think that one day you will find a gentleman who appreciates the diamond that you are and wants to marry you. I should not like to jeopardise your chance."

Ella rolled her eyes. "Stephen, I am already considered to be a spinster, there have hardly been a queue of young men eager to offer marriage and I doubt that there will be any in the future. As you say, this mission is likely to be dangerous and it might well be the case that I, or neither of us survives. I want to experience passion Stephen, if only once. I promise I shall ask nothing of you, I will not expect, demand nor want a proposal of love or marriage, but if I am to die, I want to know how it feels to be desired."

Stephen looked at her for several moments. "I thank you for your honesty, Ella," he said, before kissing her lightly on the forehead and quitting the room. Back in his own chamber, he sat on the edge of the bed with his head in his hands, her words echoing around his head, 'I will not expect, demand, nor want a proposal of love or marriage,' How was he ever going to be able to persuade Ella that she should be his wife, that he did not just want her body for one night or seven, but he wanted her as his duchess, as his equal, as his beloved wife and nothing less than that would satisfy him. They were made for each other, if only she could be persuaded to see it. Although she said that all she wanted was to experience passion before she settled into her life of spinsterhood, or death on this mission, he knew in his heart of hearts that she had feelings for him whatever she said. He knew that what they could have would be something special, something that other members of the ton could only dream about, a deep, lasting and fulfilling love, but how could he persuade her.

Stephen sat up, the only way to get through to Ella was to show her that he trusted her completely, no matter how much he ached to protect her, to ensure that she came to no harm, he must step back and allow her to make her own decisions, even though his heart would be in his mouth until they were able to return to something resembling a normal relationship. So, when they reached Yorkshire, he would say goodbye to her as she went to the old house-keeper's house and keep an eye on her from a distance as she formulated her strategy and carried it out. It was the best he could do.

CHAPTER 17

Ella barely noticed as they progressed from Stilton to The George at Stamford, The Old Bell in Derby or one of the many great inns in Doncaster for Stephen barely spoke and arranged each morning and evening for a maid to come and assist her with her clothing. It was as though he had withdrawn from her all together. Had he had his own horse she was convinced that, rather than be confined in a carriage with her, he would have preferred to have ridden alongside, despite the bitter cold and drifts of snow that almost caused the carriage to veer from the road on several occasions. By the time they reached The Black Swan at York, she was ready to scream in frustration. She had practically begged Stephen to take her to his bed with no obligation on his part and he had clearly rejected her. At the very least she would demand an explanation, her fingers traced the outline of her scar, was it the scar that had held him from taking what she had clearly been willing to give? He had said that the scars meant nothing to him, but clearly there was a distance between what he said and what he did.

After a quiet dinner of roast beef and the famous Yorkshire

pudding, Stephen stood up. "I shall escort you to your room," he announced. "Then I shall retire to mine, there are some details I need to look over before we shall arrive at Wensley tomorrow and from there, when you are ready, I shall provide suitable transport for you to travel to Castle Bolton."

"Thank you," she replied. "Mrs. Gamble knows to expect me at some point in the next few weeks, when we arrive at your estate, I shall make the necessary arrangements to go to her as soon as possible."

"There is no rush," he replied.

"Ah but if I am to procure work at the castle, I should go as soon as possible, there will be much to be done in preparation for such an important event."

"I still have reservations of how you are to pass yourself off as a servant."

"Mrs. Gamble is well known in the village, it is only a hamlet really, originally it grew up to serve the lord of the castle, she will ask at the castle. For all intents and purposes, I shall be her niece who has been orphaned and left in poverty and needs to find employment, though the earl will not care or even know who works in his castle so long as the work is done, I imagine."

As before, Stephen had arranged for a maid to help prepare her for bed, but she had no intention of going to bed until she had an explanation for Stephen's coldness towards her over the last few days. Once the noises of the inn died down and all she could hear were the creaks of the building as it settled, she draped a shawl over her nightrail, took a candle and padded down the corridor to Stephen's room. He opened the door at her first knock. "Ella, what in the blazes are you doing here?" he demanded, quickly looking down the corridor to ensure that no-one had seen her, before drawing her into the room. He had dispensed with his jacket, waistcoat and neckcloth and stood before her in his trousers and white linen shirt, his sleeves rolled up and open at the neck.

"I needed to talk to you," she said, stepping further into the room and setting her candle down on the small table.

"Then say what you have to say quickly, before someone notices that you are not in your room."

"I want to know why you have been treating me like some sort of leper for the last few days," she said, holding his gaze. "Since we left Stilton, you have hardly looked in my direction and said barely half a dozen words to me."

"I felt it best after what happened between us that we maintain a professional relationship," he replied coolly.

Ella took a breath. "I do not believe you."

He ran a hand through his hair. "Believe what you will Ella, but you must return to your room. Now."

"Why?" she persisted. "Is it because, regardless of what you said, the scars do actually revolt you, because I would rather...."

"Damnation, it is not that," he interrupted. "I have never given the scars a thought. I am merely trying to protect you, Ella."

She frowned, "Protect me? From what?"

He stepped forwards and pulled her into his arms. "From me," he said quietly as he bent his head and kissed her.

It was a kiss like no other and, as soon as his lips touched hers, her whole body felt as though it was aflame, she was aware of desire running through every vein. Her nipples tightened and her legs felt as if they were made of water. She would have sunk to the ground had Stephen not been holding her tightly against him. He had only to touch his tongue to her lips and she opened for him as he deepened the kiss. How long the kiss lasted, she could not tell, it might have been a minute, it might have been an hour, but they were both breathless when he finally raised his head.

"This," he said softly, his forehead resting on hers, "this is what I promised myself I would not do."

"But why not?" she could not help but ask. "Is it because you do not desire me enough?"

He gave her a rueful smile. "Oh, Ella, can you not tell that I desire you as much as any man has ever desired any woman? When I am in your presence I am in a permanent state of arousal. It is my greatest, my only wish to take you to my bed and make love to you until we are both exhausted."

"Then why?"

He looked up as though hoping some divine answer would help him. "Come," he said and took her hand. "Let us sit for a moment." He led her to a small sofa in front of the fire. "As I explained, I am trying to be a gentleman, if we make love Ella, when all this is over and if we both survive, I will ask for your hand because although I know you said you neither want nor expect a proposal of marriage, the fact is, that is what I want and I shall be satisfied with nothing less."

"Because you want an heir?"

"Because I want you."

"Then have me, I want you also, Stephen," she confessed.

"Then you agree, when all this is over that you will marry me?"

"Hardly the most romantic of proposals but I suppose so." She grinned.

"And hardly the most romantic of acceptances either, my lady," he grinned back, before his face became serious again. "You must be quite sure, because once we have taken this step, there is no going back, nothing will be the same again."

"I understand. Now take me to your bed, we have wasted too much time."

Stephen quickly dispensed with her shawl and night rail before pulling his shirt over his head and tossing it on the floor. Ella's eyes widened as she took in his muscular arms and sculpted torso, his muscles rippling as he lowered himself onto the bed next to her. A duke he may be and an agent of the crown, but he clearly lived a life of action. There was a faint scar running from his collar bone to his right arm. "My goodness," she said, "what happened to cause that?"

"There was a slight dispute with a 'gentleman of the road' regarding whether or not he or I would retain ownership of my purse," he replied.

"A highwayman? What happened?"

"I retained ownership of my purse, and the aforementioned gentleman will not be accosting travellers again."

Her eyes grew even wider. "You killed him?"

"Of course not, but shall we say his abilities to wield a sword or fire a pistol were significantly reduced. Now, let us not waste more time on him." He drew back the sheet and looked at her naked body. "You are quite beautiful, Ella. You take my breath away," he murmured and lowered his head to take an already peaked nipple into his mouth, while his fingers teased and caressed the other.

At this slightest touch, Ella felt desire course through her body, every inch of her skin felt alive to his touch. When his hand drifted lower and his fingers brushed her intimate part, she sighed in anticipation. "I always knew there was a passionate side to you, Ella." His quiet voice in her ear aroused her further. He stroked and caressed before sliding a finger inside. "My God, Ella, you are so wet and ready for me." He slid a second finger inside and stroked again.

Ella could not help but move against him. "Nearly, my sweet," he said with a smile.

"But what of you?" she asked, her pupils huge in her eyes. "Would you like it if I were to touch you as you touch me? Is that what is done? Please forgive my ignorance, none of our mothers survived long enough to tell us what to expect on our wedding nights."

"Oh, Ella," he almost groaned. "I would very much like it if you were to touch me. Many women of our class are taught that they must submit to their husbands, and many men are taught that only whores gain pleasure from bed sport and see their wives only as a means to secure an heir, but in my opinion, all women are as likely to find pleasure in the art of love-making as men." He quickly tugged off his trousers and under garments in one swift movement, before lying down beside her.

"May I?" she asked.

"I wish you would," he replied.

"I have never seen a naked man before."

"I should hope not." He could not help but laugh.

He hissed in pleasure as she trailed her fingers across his chest and followed the line of hair down his abdomen and towards his manhood. She grasped his cock and began to stroke. "It is so silky and yet so hard at the same time," she said.

"The hardness is what you do to me."

She bent her head. "I like it when you kiss me there, would you like me to do the same for you?"

"Dear God, you do not have to do that, but yes, I would love it."

A moan escaped as she took him into her mouth, licking and sucking as he had pleasured her. Within moments he lifted her and turned her on her back. "You are quite remarkable, but now I need to be inside you," he said, his voice raw.

She could feel the head of his cock as it nudged at her opening and he slowly slid inside. "You are so tight, I do not want to hurt you."

"I know. Please, Stephen, complete me." He heard her sharp intake of breath as he thrust fully into her. "Ella, are you all right? If I could take the pain I would, believe me."

"The pain was momentary, now I await the pleasure," she said, her voice husky with passion.

As he began to move, she instinctively matched him, thrust for thrust, he had never experienced anything like it. This woman was made for him in every way. As she neared her climax, he could feel her internal muscles flexing and she cried out as she reached her pinnacle. A moment later, he could not help but cry out as he pulled out and came in a shattering orgasm, the like of which he had never felt before with any woman.

When their breathing slowed, Ella lay on her side, propping herself on an elbow. "Why did you do that?" she asked.

He reached over and cleaned them with his shirt. "I will not risk the chance of getting you with child. I should have been more controlled and not taken you at all, but if we are unable to marry and you return carrying a child, it will be a scandal you will never recover from."

"Are you already regretting what we have just done?"

He gently brushed a curl from her face. "Of course not. Not for a second."

"Then, no more talk of control or being a gentleman. I wanted this and I too will never regret it."

Stephen settled her by his side, his arm around her and her head on his shoulder. He had not taken the whole of Ella's wall down, but perhaps a crack had appeared.

CHAPTER 18

It was dark when they finally arrived at Wensley Manor, Stephen's estate not far from Wensley and a few miles from Bolton Castle. The last part of their journey had been torturously slow due to high banks of snow on either side of the narrow roads, making it impossible for two vehicles to pass, though thankfully they had met nothing on the road. When the great door opened, the light and warmth coming from within was a welcome sight. The door opened into a spacious hall with a tiled floor in blue and white. A large oak staircase rose from the back of the room, covered in a rich blue Wilton carpet, although the walls of the hall were oak panelled, Ella could see that the walls on the staircase and the gallery above were pale with intricate plasterwork, lit by three chandeliers.

"It is quite beautiful," she said, as she took off her travelling cloak, bonnet and gloves and handed them to the waiting butler.

"My mother was responsible for the decor," Stephen replied, "though she rarely visited, claiming that this part of the world was far too cold, and given the conditions we have endured over the last couple of days, I am beginning to think she had a point.

Father used this more or less as a hunting lodge. Come into the drawing room." He turned to the butler. "I assume that there is a fire and some refreshments, Wistowe?"

"Of course, Your Grace. It is grand to have the place full of life again. We are expecting your other guests in a week or so."

"Good man." Stephan smiled at the butler. "And does Mrs. Wistowe have enough help, the house will be full when everyone arrives."

"We were able to recruit all the servants we need, though the Earl of Bolton is also seeking more servants for the masquerade on Valentine's Night. His man of business was less than happy that we had engaged so many of the villagers, but they would rather work here than in that draughty castle," he said with a laugh. "Especially as part of the masquerade is to take place in those old tunnels. Half the villagers think they're haunted, and the other half are convinced they're going to collapse, so we had no trouble engaging staff at all."

He eyed Ella with curiosity. "I've put the lady in the duchess' suite, I hope that is appropriate, Your Grace, as she is the only lady among the party."

"That is fine Wistowe," Stephen responded. "Her ladyship will need the services of a maid for the time she is here, perhaps you can suggest one?"

"There's a young maid, Barbara, who will be delighted to attend her ladyship."

Wistowe bowed and headed off down the oak panelled corridor and Stephen guided Ella to the drawing room.

"Your mother had a fine eye for decor," Ella commented as they entered the large room. The walls were painted in pale green and there was a large marble fireplace in the centre of the room with a cheerful fire blazing in the grate. Two of the walls were covered with bookcases and several sofas and armchairs were scattered around the room. An open door led to another, larger room with a pianoforte by a large window.

"Come, sit by the fire and warm yourself," Stephen said, taking the lid from some silver dishes which had been placed on the small table in front of the fireplace. "Ah, some of Mrs. Wistowe's curd tart as well as cheese, ham and fresh bread." He filled two plates as Ella poured out the steaming tea.

"I think we must begin to make a plan of action," he began, taking a bite of Wensleydale cheese. "As you may have surmised, there will be trusted agents arriving within the week."

"Then I will repair to Mrs. Gamble's cottage, although they are trusted, and no doubt, experienced agents, we cannot risk them seeing me here and unwittingly revealing who I am at Bolton Castle. Even experienced people make mistakes."

"Very well," he replied.

"And what of your servants here? Can they be trusted not to reveal that I was ever here?" she asked.

"I would trust them with my life. Wistowe and his wife have served the family for years and the other servants are all from local families who have great loyalty to the estate. My family has always ensured that those who serve us are treated well. But I understand that you had to ask."

"My own father did not enjoy the love and loyalty of the people for whom he was responsible. He was not a good landowner, neither did he care for his tenants." She looked at him, her teacup halfway to her lips. "I am glad you have no argument against my leaving to stay at the cottage."

"I have come to realise that you will do what you will do whatever I say, so no I shall not argue against you. But I will say this, we will need to meet at least regularly so that I can tell you of our plans and you can tell me what you have learned."

She nodded. "Agreed."

"There is a small waterfall in the village of Wensley, there is a path from the castle that comes out almost opposite it. The waterfall is secluded, not many know of it."

"I believe I know the one you mean, it is quite enchanting, Aunt Bette showed it to Verity and me when we were girls, we felt it was one that fairies might inhabit." She smiled at the memory; they had stayed with Aunt Bette one summer when their father had made it quite clear that he did not want them at Swallowfield. It had been the best summer of her girlhood.

"I must confess I am not comfortable with the idea of you walking down the path on your own, but I cannot risk coming too close to the castle."

"I understand. But remember, I shall be in the guise of a servant, not a lady. I doubt anyone will even notice me."

"I hope you are right." The closer they got to the mission, the more fearful for her safety he became.

Ella placed her cup and saucer down. "Let us think of something else for the moment," she said. "Would you show me around this lovely house?"

He stood and offered his arm. "Of course, I want you to feel at home here," he said. "This is the small dining room," he opened the door, again there was delicate plasterwork and a marble fireplace with a mahogany table which would seat twelve. Around the room were side tables and a fine demilune inlaid credenza along one wall. "Father used this dining room when up here hunting with his friends, on the odd occasions when he hosted a hunting party of larger proportions, he used the formal dining room which seats at least twenty and is always as cold as the devil."

"Did you and your brothers come here to hunt?" she asked.

He wrinkled his nose. "I cannot say that hunting has ever had much attraction for me. I find no pleasure in blasting at pheasants or chasing foxes until they are exhausted and torn apart by dogs."

"Me either, I have always enjoyed spending time with

animals," Ella replied, "they are so much more forgiving and loving than humans."

"Except cats," he replied with a laugh, "cats are supremely indifferent to us however much we try to please them." Ella squeezed his arm, it was good to hear him laugh, it was a sound she had not heard in a few days, and it would be good to take his mind away from the upcoming mission, even if only for a short time. It occurred to her that the success or failure of the mission was entirely Stephen's responsibility and should he fail, the consequences would be far reaching and dire.

"I have an idea," she said. "Until your colleagues arrive in the next few days, let us take this time for ourselves, of course we must not be too distracted from what is at hand, but time to prepare and make plans could also be a time for us to get to know each other again." For all the world, she could not have explained why she said this, but somehow it was important to her that Stephen see her as she truly was.

"I should very much like that," he replied, reaching down and caressing her cheek with the back of his hand. "The stars have never seemed aligned where we are concerned, and we should make the most of any opportunity fate allows us."

"Then tomorrow, we shall build a snowman, we cannot let all this snow go to waste." She laughed at his bemused expression.

"Very well and I shall instruct my coachman to prepare the old sleigh, so that we may take a ride around the estate."

"Perfect," she replied with a smile.

"And now I shall escort you to your chamber."

"Will you join me?" she asked, shyly.

"If that is what you wish," he replied, his eyes darkening.

"It is."

"Then who am I to deny a lady what she desires?"

Once again, Stephen's mother's taste was evident in the delicate furnishing and decor of the duchess' rooms. The walls and ceiling were painted a delicate, pale green with the drapes and bed hangings a darker shade of green velvet with the palest of pink linings. Two chairs stood by the marble fireplace and each window had a seat for its owner to enjoy an unrivalled view over the formal garden and the park beyond. Between the two large windows a mirror was attached to the wall and throughout there were tables and footstools scattered. One door opened to what Ella could see was a room set aside specifically for bathing and another appeared to be a whole room set aside for the storage of clothing, the final door, she surmised, led to the ducal chamber.

Ella was surprised to find that her belongings had already been unpacked and her night rail and dressing robe laid out on the bed. Almost before she had taken in her surroundings there was a quiet knock on the door and a young maid entered. "I've been sent to 'elp yer undress yer ladyship," the girl said as she bobbed a curtsey.

"Thank you. What is your name?" Ella asked.

"Barbara, yer ladyship."

"Have you worked for the duke for a long time?" Ella enquired as Barbara deftly unlaced her gown and slipped it over her head.

"Not really yer ladyship. Me mam worked for 'is mother, lovely lady she was, the old duchess. There 'asn't been much call for a lady's maid since she died. I've been workin' as a 'ousemaid, but truth to tell I want to be a real lady's maid, I promise I'll work 'ard for yer." She deftly drew Ella's night rail over her head and held the dressing robe for Ella to slip into it.

"I am sure you will, Barbara," Ella replied with a smile.

"Is there anythin' else yer ladyship?"

"No thank you Barbara, I shall see you in the morning," Ella replied. Barbara was going to be more help than she realised as a model for her role as maidservant.

Stephen paused in the doorway, drinking in the sight. Ella was sitting at the writing desk, her quill moving rapidly across the paper, her lips puckered as she concentrated on whatever it was she was writing, the light from the fire highlighted the auburn lights in her hair which she had left loose. "Do you never stop?" he asked, coming into the room.

She turned and smiled at him. "Thinking? Rarely, there is so much to think about."

He stalked towards her, his banyan flowing around him, his feet bare on the Aubusson carpet. "Tonight, Ella," he said, taking the quill from her grasp and laying it on the escritoire. "Tonight, dearest Ella, I don't want you to think at all, I want you to feel. I want you to empty your mind of all distracting thoughts and concentrate entirely on what we are going to do. Think of the touch of my hands on your skin. Think of my fingers as they caress your breasts. I can see that excites you already, I can see your nipples beginning to peak. That is it, Ella, feel it, embrace it. Imagine how my mouth feels as it makes its way down your body until it finds the place we both know will give you supreme pleasure, imagine how you will feel when I am deep inside you."

"Sweet heavens, Stephen," she gasped, her eyes wide, "I am almost ready to come to fulfilment, and you have not laid a single finger on me."

His laugh was low and sensuous. "Then the sooner you are out of those garments and naked in my arms the better," he said, scooping her in his arms and striding toward his own chamber. Within moments the time for words was over and all that could be heard were sighs and moans.

CHAPTER 19

When he awoke, Stephen was surprised to find the space beside him was empty and, judging by the coolness of the sheets, had been for some time. Ella was an early riser, that much he knew, but he had thought that their night-time activities might have tired her enough for her to have stayed a little longer, especially as he had anticipated making love to her again this morning. He smiled at the memory of their night together, now that Ella had been introduced to the joys of love-making, she had engaged in it with passion, he had nearly died of pleasure when she had taken his cock into her mouth, or when he had lifted her on top and she had ridden him, hard. There was no doubt in his mind that in bed, they were extremely suited, but that was not all, he loved her ready wit and intelligence, the way she could hold her own in a discussion and put forth logical arguments to support her point. He noticed her gracious and pleasant manner with the servants, she would make an ideal duchess, his ideal duchess. All he had to do was to persuade her of it.

Sighing, he got out of bed, donned a robe and went in search of Ella. The room was empty save for a plump maid who was tying back the bed hangings.

"Do you know where her ladyship is?" he asked.

The woman stopped what she was doing and bobbed a curtsey, keeping her head down as all the young maids seemed to do. "No Yer Grace, I ain't seen nobody. I was just told to come and tidy 'er ladyship's room. P'raps she went down to break 'er fast."

Stephen paused by the door as he headed back to his room. "Are you new? I do not recall seeing you before."

"Ay Yer Grace, I started this mornin'."

"And what is your name?"

"Ellie Yer Grace, short for 'elen. I'm named for me granny. God rest 'er soul, though she were a right termigant an' no mistake. She'd bite yer ears off as soon as look at yer. In the old days, they'd probably 'ave burned 'er for a witch." She lowered her head again. "Sorry, Yer Grace, I shouldn't be blatherin' on."

He nodded and turned but stopped at the sound of laughter. "What the devil?" he said as the 'maid' took off her mob cap and Ella's luxuriant hair cascaded down her back. "There," she said, taking a cloth and wiping the smear of dirt from her face. "I think that proves that I should be able to pass as a maid, especially in a house where no-one knows me."

"You minx," he said, but he could not help but grin.

"You see," she said, reaching under her skirt and removing some padding, "many people of our class do not notice servants at all and some demand that they face the wall if they come into contact with them. One duke as I recall even had corridors built into the walls of his house so that he never had to see servants at all. Others know the names and faces of their personal servants, butlers, valets and ladies' maids but the rest of the people in their household might as well be or indeed are complete strangers to them."

Stephen pursed his lips. "I had not thought of that."

"At least you knew that the 'new maid' was not familiar."

"That I did, but I genuinely had no idea it was you. However, I have a day of pleasure planned for us and I do not wish to waste a single second more, so summon your real maid and dress warmly."

"A day of pleasure." Ella smiled and licked her lips.

His voice deepened. "Oh, there will be all kinds of pleasure my lady, make no mistake." He blew her a kiss and disappeared into his own chamber.

Dressed in a warm dark emerald green woollen dress with matching pelisse and small brimmed bonnet trimmed with white swansdown, Ella was delighted when she saw the one-horse sleigh outside the front door.

"Oh, this is perfect," she said as Stephen helped her in and tucked a warm blanket around them both. "Such a pity it did not snow like this for Christmas."

"January and February are often the harshest months," he said, expertly guiding the sleigh away, "in this part of the world at least." Within minutes they were sliding smoothly across the park and through a small wood.

"Do you have a destination in mind?" she asked.

He turned to her and smiled. "Indeed, I do and I think you will find it enchanting."

Although there was less snow under the shelter of the trees, the sleigh ran smoothly on the wide trail. The weather had remained very cold since the first snow had fallen and the trees maintained their snowy shawls.

"It is quite magical," Ella said, her eyes darting from left to right. "I do not want to miss a thing." They rode in companionable silence until the trail opened out and they approached a small lake beside which was a cabin with welcoming candles in the window and smoke curling from the chimney. "Oh, she gasped, I had not expected anything like this."

"We always called it the secret lake," Stephen explained. "It is particularly beautiful in summer when it is covered in water lilies."

"It is beautiful now," she replied. "It is the perfect winter scene."

Stephen helped her down and untied the horse, leading it to a shelter adjacent to the cabin.

"There is a natural dip, and we think the lake is filled by an underground spring, but we have never managed to find its source. The lake itself is quite deep and if you look up there," he pointed to the overhanging limestone cliff, "when there has been a lot of rain, there is a waterfall."

"Oh yes, and look, there is water frozen in its cascade," she said.

"My father had the cabin built so that we could have picnics in the summer. Come." He held out his hand. "Let us see what awaits us within."

The cabin was rustic, the walls were formed from logs and the small windows had bright curtains, a cheerful fire burned in the hearth and food had been laid out on the table under the window.

"This is delightful," Ella said, looking around her, "it is like the house in the tale of Goldilocks, and the three bears Mrs. Clayton told us when we were girls.

He chuckled, the sound warm. "I can assure you there are no bears likely to come and interrupt our meal. I can also assure you that we shall not be eating porridge either," he added. "Come, I find the fresh air has given me an appetite. He removed the white table linen to reveal ham, freshly baked bread, a selection of cheese, a carafe of wine, fruit and a pound cake.

"I had not realised I was hungry," Ella said when she had finished, "until I saw the food. Your cook bakes the most marvellous bread and cakes."

"It is the one thing I miss when I am abroad," he admitted.

"I am sure the chefs of the continent are more than capable," she teased.

"Oh, that they are, but there is nothing like the smell and taste of home cooking. You have a crumb," he said, gently brushing the side of her mouth with his thumb before leaning forward and capturing her lips with his own, leaving her wanting more when he drew back. He stood up. "Much as I would like nothing more than to spend the afternoon making love to you, time is passing. Would you care for a stroll around the lake? We shall not tarry long because it will soon be dusk and it would be best if we were not driving home in the dark. The horse is sure footed, but the tracks are uneven and I do not want to risk tipping the sleigh, let alone the fact that once the sun goes down, it will be considerably colder."

They walked along the water's edge, the snow crunching under their boots. "I do love winter," Ella said, "everything looks clean and magical."

"It does cover up a multitude of sins," he agreed, "until it melts and becomes a dirty slush."

"Have you no romance in your soul?"

He pondered for a while. "Perhaps where you are concerned, but otherwise, no. Life has taught me that romance is an expensive and sometimes dangerous notion. It is better to be realistic, that way, one is rarely disappointed. For example, your admiration of a snowy winter scene is based on the assumption that you will be warm and well fed throughout the winter months because that is what you have experienced. For a farmer, the situation is rather more concerning. Will the crops wither and die in the cold weather and will he be able to feed his family? For the truly poor the winter is a time of survival, both in terms of warmth and food. It is all a matter of perspective."

She wrinkled her brow. "You are right of course, I have the privilege of enjoying the winter and returning to warmth and comfort."

"The important thing is that those who are so privileged take care of those who are not, but many landowners do little for their tenants or those in need on their estates."

She looked up at him with admiration. "I have a feeling that like Elliott, you take your responsibilities to the poor seriously."

He smiled down at her. "I do what I can," he replied, simply. "Now, I think we must make tracks back to the cabin and return to the house."

When they arrived back at the house, the butler greeted them at the door. "Two gentlemen have arrived Your Grace, a Mr. Thomas and Mr. Williams, they said you were expecting them, but their journey did not take as long as expected and they apologise for arriving early. Rooms have been prepared for them in the guest wing, and they await your presence in the library."

"Thank you Wistowe." He turned to Ella. "I had hoped that our time together here would be longer, but it seems that is not to be."

"I take it these are some of your men," she replied. He nodded.

"Then tomorrow I shall depart for Castle Bolton."

"You do not have to go so soon," he protested.

"We agreed that I should not meet with your agents so that neither of us was in danger of giving the other away," she pointed out. "In any case, Mrs. Gamble is expecting me at any time."

"Now who is the realist?" he asked, quirking an eyebrow.

Ella quietly slipped up the stairs to her chamber and packed the few things she would need for her performance as a servant. Two shabby dresses, a woollen shawl and a worn pair of boots as well as woollen stockings and two caps. If she was to work in the castle as she hoped, they would no doubt provide her with livery. Her thoughts constantly turned to Stephen, he was a man she could fall in love with, had fallen in love with. He was honourable, kind, handsome beyond belief and he made her feel and want things she thought she had long stopped hoping for. Of course, the situation they found themselves in was far from normal and it may be that if and when normal life returned, she might feel differently.

When Barbara came to help her get ready for bed, she confessed that she would be leaving early in the morning.

"I know yer ladyship, the master told me, 'e said I'm to go with yer and not let yer out of me sight."

"The duke told you what?" Ella could not believe her ears.

"'Is Grace told me you're doin' somethin' important fer t'king an' I'm 'onoured to be 'elpin'. 'E said you're ter pass yerself off as a maid. Well, I can 'elp yer with that." The girl grinned. "It'll be t'most exciting' thing that ever 'appens to me to be sure."

"Did the duke tell you that it could also be dangerous?" Ella asked.

Barbara's grin got wider. "'E did. Fancy me bein' able to 'elp t'king. An' don't yer worry about me yer ladyship, I 'ave five brothers, I learnt long ago when ter keep me mouth shut an' 'ow to take care o' meself."

Ella could not help but return the grin. "There are one or two moves I can teach you that might come in useful," she said, "and I will be very glad of your company."

Hours later, when she was quite sure that the house was silent and all were in their chambers, she knocked on Stephen's door and walked in. He was sitting at the writing desk in the window alcove, making notes. He had, as usual, taken off his jacket, waistcoat and neckcloth and rolled up his sleeves. He looked up and smiled when he saw her. "I was going to come to you myself, but I needed to get my thoughts down on paper before I forgot any of the details my colleagues reported to me."

"What were you thinking, putting Barbara in harm's way?" she began.

"Barbara is loyal and brave, I wanted to ensure that you had someone else on the inside that you could trust," he explained. "That being said, she is also entirely trustworthy."

"But..."

He held up a hand. "I have listened to what you said about the lives of women being made small by men and I conclude that you are right. Like the rest of my sex, I have not considered the potential that women have so now I am putting my trust in the two of you, and I know that trust is not misplaced."

"Thank you," she said, "Barbara and I will not let you down."

He rose and walked towards her, beginning to unfasten the buttons on his shirt. "And now, tonight I do not want to think of what we are about to embark on, I do not want to think of anything other than what is to happen between us" he inclined his head " in that bed."

CHAPTER 20

It was still dark when the unmarked carriage discharged its passengers at the end of the lane leading to Castle Bolton. Barbara and Ella walked in silence and approached the only house with a candle in the window as had been arranged with Mrs. Gamble. Due to the snow, their boots made no sound as they walked up the short path and knocked on the door which was opened immediately and they were ushered in. Mrs. Gamble was a small, slim woman with faded auburn hair almost all hidden by a lace cap. Her brown dress was covered by a large apron on which she wiped her hands.

"Come in my dears and get warm, it's cold enough to freeze a brass monkey's tail off. I've tea brewing and porridge if you're hungry."

"Thank you, Mrs. Gamble. It is good of you to put us up," Ella said.

"It's no bother," the older woman replied. "Truth to tell, I'll be rather glad of the company, especially now the weather's turned, the nights are long and dark"

The two younger women looked at each other. "I am not sure

we shall be able to spend too much time here," Ella said. "We might even have to stay at the castle."

"No, you won't my dears. There's such a to do at the castle what with the new earl's Valentine's Ball, there's workers over here from all over Yorkshire, making the place habitable for his visitors that there's no room. I arranged with Mrs. Heaton, the housekeeper that you would stay here. It's only a short step to the castle from the village. When the castle was built the village grew up around it to service it and they didn't want their servants too far away in those days."

"Thank you for organising it Mrs. Gamble," Ella replied.

"It's just such a shame that a lady such as you should be brought so low that she has to work as a servant," the old housekeeper said, wiping her eyes on her apron."

"You did not mention that to Mrs. Heaton?" Ella asked, anxiously.

"Of course not, I said you were my niece who had fallen on hard times, the story we agreed. But," she added looking at Barbara, "I'm not sure what to say about the other young lady."

Ella thought for moment. "We said that I am your sister's child and am now orphaned and it emerged that when my father died, he had many debts which we did not know about. Barbara could have been our maid of all work who would have been thrown out when the bailiffs came to re-possess the house. I insisted that she come with me and we are both happy to work at the castle. How does that sound?" In truth, it was not so dissimilar to what had actually happened to her when her father died.

"I suppose it will be all right, and to be honest, there is so much to do, they'll no doubt welcome another pair of hands. Now, let's have some tea and porridge, I'll get you settled in your room, you'll have to share and then we'll go up to the castle."

"It's very big," Barbara observed as they approached the imposing keep.

"It was built in the heyday of castle building in the fourteenth century," Ella explained. "It was meant to withstand attack from all sides, though as far as I remember from my earlier tour, it has never actually been attacked, but Mary, Queen of Scots was kept a prisoner here for a time."

Barbara's eyes widened. "Really, 'ere?"

Ella nodded. "Apparently, according to the old Earl, it was here that she learned to speak English, she spoke French, Latin and Scottish, but no English when she arrived."

"Well, bless me," Barbara exclaimed. "Fancy not knowin' 'ow to speak English."

"I think you will find that a lot of people do not." Ella smiled as she pulled on the metal bell pull to announce their arrival.

The massive oak door opened, and a small man looked them over. "Mrs. Gamble to see Mrs. Heaton with the two new maids," the older lady said.

The man nodded and opened the door. "Follow me," he said and set off quickly down the stone corridor, their footsteps echoing as they kept up with him. Eventually they reached a smaller door down which was a staircase, lit by sconces on the wall. "Blimey, it's like somethin' out of Robin 'ood," Barbara said, her eyes wide.

"Mrs. Heaton's down there in the kitchen," he said, motioning for them to go down. "E's not very welcoming is 'e?" Barbara ventured as they made their way down. "That's Wilkins, Mrs. Gamble explained. "He's been here since Adam was a lad."

"I thought I recognised him," Ella said, quietly. "Let us hope he does not recognise me."

"No danger of that," the older woman replied. "When you saw him, you were a young girl, dressed as a lady. Now you're most definitely a woman who has to work for her crust. I doubt that your own father would recognise you."

"I doubt that too, Mrs. Gamble, but for entirely different reasons," Ella replied, remembering that her father had never wanted to look at her and scarcely so much as glanced at her.

"Well then," a woman's voice greeted them, "I take it these are the two lasses you thought able to cope with the work here." A plump woman walked towards them, wiping her hands on her apron.

"Aye, Mrs. Heaton," Mrs. Gamble replied. "They're good girls and know the meaning of hard work."

"They'll need it," the other woman replied. "What with builders and carpenters here for weeks, you've no idea of the dust they've kicked up, I swear some if it's from the time Queen Mary was here. Anyway, we're to be ready for the beginning of February when his lordship's guests start to arrive. Why he wanted to have this do for Valentine's Day I don't know, but there it is. So," she looked at the two young women, "there's plenty of work getting the rooms ready and you'll have to be able to work through the masquerade and after, we'll see if there's enough for you to be taken on permanently. Does that suit?"

"Yes, ma'am," Ella replied, giving a brief bob and pulling Barbara down to do the same.

"Very well, I shall expect you at seven sharp in the morning, you'll get half an hour to eat and finish at sunset. You'll have one Sunday off a month and a half day every other week, though you may be asked to do more hours if there's work to be done. You'll be paid one shilling a week, and breakages or other damage will be taken from your wages, is that understood?"

"Yes ma'am," Ella replied. Barbara nodded.

"Bloody 'ell," Barbara exclaimed as they left the castle, "them wages wouldn't keep a mouse in cheese. The Duke pays 'is maids a guinea a month and they work less hours and get a bed and fed.

'E's a good man is the duke, and 'e's still payin' me while I do this job."

"The duke is indeed a generous man," Ella replied, and it was true, she could not dispute it, he had never shown her anything but kindness and she had thrown that kindness back in his face, thinking he only saw her as a charity case, to be rescued from a life of spinsterhood. Or perhaps it was his overdeveloped sense of duty that motivated him, he put duty to king and country above all things, mayhap he had become so used to doing the right thing that had motivated him to propose marriage. She shook her head, she could not think of that now. What she must plan was how to get into the Earl's study so that she may find something of use for their mission.

Both girls were up early and presented themselves at the castle before seven, it was still dark and they had to carry lanterns to pick their way down the narrow lane to the castle.

"Glad to see you're on time," Mrs. Heaton said as she opened the small side door they had been told to use. "Now then, you," she nodded to Barbara, "are to go upstairs to the master bedroom. The carpenters have finished building his lordship's bed and the walls have been painted, but there's too much dust and dirt to hang the linens, so I want it spotless by the end of the day. Freddy will show you the way." She handed Barbara several cloths, soap, a broom and a mop. "Freddy will carry the pails of water for you," she added. "Freddy," she spoke to the large young man sitting at the table eating a large slice of bread and butter, "fetch two pails and fill them with hot water from the copper and take them up to the master's bedroom."

"You, Ellie, is it?" Ella nodded. "You're to go to the library, the carpenters have finished with the new bookshelves, you're to polish the shelves and help put the books back. There'll also be the other furniture in the room to polish, and the windows will need cleaning. I don't know how we're ever going to get rid of all this dust." She handed Ella a pot of beeswax and an earthenware jug of vinegar as well as several cloths. "No slacking now, I cannot abide laziness." was her parting shot.

"Oh, my goodness," Ella murmured as she took in the newly made shelves which rose from floor to ceiling. "I 'ope the earl 'as plenty of books to fill 'em."

"Indeed, he does," a deep voice responded. She started. "I'm sorry, Sir, I didn't know anyone was 'ere." She dropped a curtsey to the young man who was almost hidden among the boxes in the centre of the room.

"And who might you be?" he asked.

"Ellie, My Lord Sir, Ellie." She paused for a beat before adding, "Grange, Sir, one of t'new maids." The less she said, the better. The man could be a senior footman or under butler, he was well dressed enough, or he might even be the Earl, she had not seen him since she was a child.

"Well, Grange, better get on with it, begin with the shelves," he replied before consulting his pocket watch and quitting the room.

"Yes, My Lord, Sir," she said to his rapidly retreating back.

It took two hours of dusting before Ella could begin to apply the polish, but by noon the shelves were more or less free of dust and the room smelled of sweet beeswax. She looked at the boxes and decided to wait until whoever the rather abrupt young man was, returned, presumably there was some system that he no doubt wanted to use to arrange the books. She turned her attention to the rather large, impressive desk, if there were to be any documents which might be of use, they would surely be in here. Of course, the desk was locked, but that did not deter her. Retrieving a hairpin from under her cap, and keeping an eye on the door, she set to work to unlock the drawers. It proved to be easier than she had expected, the lock gave way with a satisfying click. She did not bother to look for anything in the actual drawers, any conspirator worth his salt would not leave anything incriminating where it might be easily found. However, like her father's desk, she reasoned that there would be some sort of secret compartment, and she was not disappointed.

CHAPTER 21

Fortunately, the bundle of papers was small enough to push into her bodice, she had just managed to re-lock the drawer and pick up her cloth when the door opened.

"What are you doing at the desk?" It was the same man she had met earlier.

"Just polishin' it my lord. Mrs. 'eaton said I was to polish t' shelves and t'furniture and 'elp with putting the books back, but I didn't know where to put 'em so I started on t' desk," she explained.

"The desk is fine, leave it. You may help me put the books in order."

"I'll be 'appy to my lord, if you pass 'em to me I'll put 'em on t'shelves," Ella replied, beginning to climb the ladder.

They worked in silence for a moment or two before he said, "Wait. You are putting the books upside down." His eyes narrowed. "Can you read girl?"

Ella adopted what she hoped was an appropriate expression. "No, my lord, my father thought learning was not for t'likes of us, not that 'e could afford for me to go to school in any case." If he thought she was illiterate, so much the better, he might be less careful with his documents. "I can write my name," she added with pride.

"You do not strike me as stupid girl, just make sure that you place the books with the lettering at the top."

"I can do that my lord," she said, peering at the book in her hand and placing it carefully, the correct way up and adjusting the others. "There my lord, is that what you meant?"

He glanced up and nodded.

They worked through until it was beginning to grow dark. "Is that all, My Lord?" Ella asked as she placed the last book on the lowest shelf.

"That is all, you may go."

"Thank you, My Lord." She bobbed a curtsey and left the room, he had rebuffed all her attempts at conversation, in fact each time he had looked at her it was almost as though he saw right through her, he barely registered her presence other than mechanically putting his books on the shelves.

"Now then," Mrs. Heaton asked as she and Barbara began to put their cloaks on to return to the cottage, "how did you get on?"

"T'bed chamber's finished," Barbara reported, "and ready for t'linens tomorrow".

"Good work." Mrs. Heaton nodded before turning to Ella. "And you?"

"T'shelves are done and I 'elped his lordship to put t'books back, but 'e didn't want me to polish the rest of t'furniture."

Mrs. Heaton frowned. "That wasn't his lordship, he won't arrive for another few days, that was one of his new friends, Lord Horatio Oliver. He's become quite the fixture around here, however, he isn't the owner of the castle and as the housekeeper I decide what tasks my maids are allocated, so tomorrow, you will finish in the library and then I have special work for both of you."

"Well, that was interestin'," Barbara remarked as they made their way down the lane. "Yer sound more Yorkshire than I do, but I don't think Mrs. 'eaton is overly fond o' that Lord Oliver."

"No, indeed," Ella replied, "and having spent the afternoon with him, I can quite see why."

The cottage was cosy after their walk and both women were grateful to warm themselves by the fire. Mrs. Gamble had made an excellent stew, and both were hungry after the day's work. They had just finished eating when there was a sharp knock at the door. "See who's at the door, would you? Not that I'm expecting visitors," Mrs. Gamble said as she took their dishes into the scullery.

"I'll 'elp with the washin' up," Barbara said, following the older woman.

Ella's eyes widened in surprise when she saw Stephen casually leaning against the door frame. "What are you doing here?" she asked.

He strode inside. "I wanted to know how you got on today and frankly, Ella, I cannot bear the thought of you in that place where I cannot protect you," he said, before sweeping her into his arms and kissing her.

They were both breathing heavily when he stepped back and rested his forehead against hers. "I have wanted to do that since the moment I said good-bye to you," he admitted, with a smile.

"I have missed you," she said softly, revelling in the feeling of being in his arms. "But is it not dangerous for you to be here, you might have been seen."

"My horse is well hidden in a shelter at the end of the lane. I walked the last mile or so and I am hardly dressed as befits a duke."

She stepped back and looked at him. "Indeed, no-one would

mistake you for a member of the ton," she said and could not help but laugh. His brown coat was patched as were the green trousers and his hat looked as though it had done service at the Battle of Waterloo. "The only thing that might give you away is the state of your boots, far too polished for such a poor specimen."

"Ah, there are some things I am not prepared to compromise and the groom's feet (from whom I borrowed these clothes) are smaller than mine. Now," he said, moving to the table and motioning for Ella to join him. "Tell me what happened today."

"A lot of dusting and polishing," she replied, taking a seat next to him. "But I did find this," she fished the papers from the front of her bodice. "I have not had time to look at them."

"Where did you find them?"

"They were in a secret compartment in the earl's desk. There's a man called Lord Oliver who seems to have a great deal of power in the castle. Mrs. Heaton, the housekeeper clearly does not like him. As far as I could tell, the earl is not in residence yet. Anyway, I was set to clean the bookshelves in the library and polish the furniture, Lord Oliver clearly did not want me anywhere near the desk."

"Then how did you manage to get hold of these?"

She gave him a sly grin. "Ah, a little trick with a hairpin and good timing".

"I do not want you taking unnecessary risks," he admonished.

"I shall put them back tomorrow, Lord Oliver will not even know they are missing," she reassured him.

"He will if he looks for them this evening."

"Well, we shall face that problem if it arises tomorrow. Now, what is in them?"

Stephen carefully unfolded the papers. "It would seem that your efforts are in vain," he said, "the pages appear to be blank."

She shook her head. "I think we both know that there is some message on this paper written in invisible ink, and we both know that heat will reveal its contents."

He looked at her with respect. "Once again I am sure that you are possibly the best agent we never had."

He reached for the candlestick. "The trick is not to hold the flame too close so that the paper gets hot enough to ignite, here," he fished a notebook and pencil from his pocket. "When I read out the contents, will you please write it down so that we have a copy."

Ella nodded and opened the notebook.

There was a pause before he began, "My God, it is a list of the names of the conspirators." He began to read them out. The second sheet contained the names of those who were to be sent to the new industrial cities to whip up unrest among the workers, the third, the factories, mines, shipyards and ironworks which were to be the targets. The final sheet gave details of where and when mass protests were to be held. What you have discovered is pure gold," he said, laying down the final sheet and watching as the writing began, once again, to disappear.

"I wonder why, given the incendiary nature of this information, they did not bother to encrypt these documents," she mused.

"I would hazard a guess that whoever wrote them believed them to be safe within the confines of the castle, perhaps each conspirator will be given only a small piece of information at the masked ball with only the orders of what they are to do. What you have discovered would appear to be the master plan."

"There is no mention here of the so-called rightful Tudor heir," she pointed out.

"Mayhap that is something they are keeping secret and will only use to quell the mob if the country becomes unstable. Whatever happens, you have done your country proud, but we must now think of a way to get you safely away from here."

"Oh no you do not, Stephen, Bolton Castle has more secrets,

and I intend to find them. I want to know who this Lord Oliver is and why he seems to be in control of much of what is going on there. Also, Mrs. Heaton said that there was special work for Barbara and me tomorrow."

"I suppose arguing with you on this point would be a waste of both my breath and time."

"Indeed."

"Then just be careful, do not do anything reckless either which endangers your safety or puts the mission at risk."

"I shall be the soul of discretion," she assured him.

"You will be the death of me," he said, pulling her once again into an embrace. "I cannot bear the thought of losing you. When this is over..."

She placed a finger on his lips. "We shall talk of the future when we know we have one. Now go, Barbara and I have to be up early, not like you nobles who may lay in bed all morning," she teased.

"Minx." He kissed her again before disappearing into the night.

Sleep did not come easily, and Ella's thoughts were in a whirl as she hugged her pillow. Could it be that there might be a future for her and Stephen? She had not seen him since she had rejected his proposal years ago, as a wealthy man in possession of one of the highest titles in the land, he could have had the pick of each year's debutantes with which to sire an heir, and yet he had not married. Could it really be that he harboured feelings for her after all these years as she did for him? It was all too easy to imagine that he was in love with her and that it was not too late for them to marry and raise the family she had always dreamed of but never dared to hope for. She gave herself a mental shake; much as she wanted to allow her imagination to wander down these pleasant lanes, it was foolish. They were embroiled in a mission which heightened the senses of all kinds, it could well be that their attraction towards each other was a result of the situation. If, when all this was over, the attraction still existed and had not melted away like morning mist, then, perhaps there might be a future for them, but until then she could only dream, and that was dangerous.

CHAPTER 22

"Now," Mrs. Heaton said as they removed their cloaks the following morning, "as you know, we've visitors arriving for this masked ball the master's throwing, so I shall need you both to do some extra work. You both did well yesterday, and Mrs. Gamble assures me that you can both be trusted."

Both young women nodded. "You no doubt don't know, why should you? But underneath the castle is a series of tunnels and caverns and the young lord wants to hold the ball down there. The lasses from the village don't like going down there but they must be cleaned and made ready for the occasion so you," she nodded to Barbara, "I should like you to go down there with a couple of footmen, good boys, and make sure it's fit for the entertainment. The walls have been whitewashed so it's a case of making sure the floors are clean and helping to set up some sort of stage for the musicians and tables for the dinner."

"That seems like a lot o' responsibility," Barbara said.

"And you shall be paid a little extra, though I shall expect both of you to help out on the night of the ball as well."

Ella smiled, this was perfect.

"I have a special job for you, Ellie," Mrs. Heaton went on, "there's a young master in the south tower staying here. Lord Oliver has engaged a tutor for him, but the lad's struggling to settle in. For some reason, his lordship wants to meet with the tutor so you will sit with the lad."

Ella schooled her face to remain neutral. "Of course, Mrs. 'eaton, but should I finish polishing in t'library first? The shelves are done, it's just t'other furniture that needs fettling."

"Aye lass, finish that now."

Ella let out a breath, had she not been able to return the documents, the mission would have, no doubt been compromised.

She had just replaced the documents, locked the desk and picked up her cleaning cloth when the door burst open.

"You again," Lord Oliver exclaimed. "I distinctly told you to keep away from the desk."

"Sorry, my lord, but Mrs. 'eaton was definite about t'furniture being polished before t'master gets here," Ella explained.

"Do not dare to be impertinent, girl," he raged. "Get out of my sight and consider yourself lucky that I do not send you packing."

"But Mrs. 'eaton said..."

"Out," he roared.

Ella hid a small smile as she left the room, Lord Oliver was exactly the sort of noble who did not deserve the title, and she would take great pleasure in taking him down more than a peg or two. Why the Earl of Bolton tolerated him she could not imagine.

"Lord Oliver doesn't want me anywhere near the furniture in t'library," she reported to the housekeeper. 'Shall I 'elp Barbara if I'm not needed yet for t'young master?"

"Yes, that will be a help, but you'll be needed this afternoon,

I'll send a lad to fetch you. How his lordship thinks we can get all this done before this ball I don't know."

The tunnels were larger and more far reaching than she remembered, as far as she recalled there were several stories of why they were dug, one was to provide work for the men of the village when times were hard and the harvest had failed and the other was that they emerged in Leyburn as an escape route for if the castle was besieged. There were flaming torches in sconces along the walls as she made her way to the central chamber where she heard Barbara laughing.

"So 'ow many are we to set the table for?" Barbara asked the footman who was assembling the table as Ella found them.

"Twenty was what I was told," he replied.

"Their food is going to be cold by the time it gets 'ere," Ella observed, coming further into the circular room.

"That's what I said." Barbara grinned. "Did yer finish early in t'library?"

Ella wrinkled her nose. "Lord Oliver was quite definite that he didn't want anyone near t'desk, though I can't see for the life of me why he should be bothered, given that it's not even 'is desk," she ventured, wondering if the footman might take the bait.

"Aye, 'e's an odd one and no mistake,' the young man said. "Sometimes it seems as though 'e's the earl 'ere, but rich folk 'ave strange ways as my mother used to say," he paused, "some do say that it's 'is money that's paid for all t'renovations."

"Well, that would explain 'im walking around like he owns the place," Ella replied. The young man said no more, and they worked putting out chairs and tables until a young man appeared. "Mrs. Heaton says you're to come back now," he said.

Before she opened the door to the room at the top of the south tower, she could hear a child's cries. Pushing open the door she saw a small boy cowering in the corner as a tall, young man brandished a cane. "You simpleton," he shouted, red in the face, "it is not difficult. You have had all week to learn the names of the kings and queens of England." He raised the cane. "And if you do not know them by tonight, you shall have nothing but bread and water until you do."

"Sir," Ella exclaimed, "Mrs. 'eaton has sent me to look after t'child while you meet with 'is lordship. I believe 'is lordship is waiting."

The young man lowered the cane. "And who the devil are you?"

"Ellie, Sir, one of the new maids. I was ordered to sit with t'boy when you're too busy," she explained, adding, "Mrs. 'eaton says you are a busy man with much to do."

"That much is true, well," he said as he straightened up. "Do you know your letters girl?" She shook her head.

"Why am I surrounded by dunderheads?" he huffed. "No matter, the boy may practise his writing." He turned to the child. "I expect to see a clean copy of your letters when I return, in a neat hand with no ink blotches, do you understand?"

"Yes Sir," the child mumbled, wiping his face on his sleeve.

"Speak up, boy. When you take your place you shall have to address a roomful of people and must be heard clearly."

"Yes, Sir," the boy repeated, a little more loudly. "You may use the cane if there is any slacking," the tutor said before he turned and left the room.

"I'm Ellie," Ella said, coming further into the room. "What is your name?"

"Harry," the boy replied.

"How old are you, 'arry?" Ella asked.

"Seven," he replied.

"Well, 'arry, why don't we get on with the writing and then mayhap we can go outside and play in the garden?"

The child looked horrified. "I am not allowed out. Mr. Marks would beat me again."

"Mr. Marks is your tutor?"

Harry nodded. "I hate it here, I hate Mr. Marks. I want to go home. I want my mother and father." His lips trembled.

"Of course you do, but you must be here for a reason," Ella suggested.

"I am not allowed to say," Harry answered quickly.

"Well, then." Ellie smiled brightly, changing the subject. "What say we get through your letters as quickly as possible, then we might 'ave time to play a game?"

With a little encouragement, Harry formed his letters and sounded them out to Ella who sounded them back to him.

"I learned my letters in dame school in our village," Harry confessed, "but Mr. Marks says that I shall have to sign important documents so my writing must be better."

Ella gave him a warm smile. "I think it's very good, young Sir. Not a blotch in sight. Now what shall we play?"

"There is a chess set, but I don't know how to play," Harry replied.

"Well, as it 'appens, I do," Ella said, adding, "my father used to carve them." Which was not true, he did collect them and had a collection of jade sets from China which, like all the other items of value, had been sold to pay his debts.

Ella set up the board and taught Harry the basic moves, he proved to be a quick learner, and she began to think that the reason he struggled with what Mr. Marks was teaching him was because he was terrified of the man and the man was a bully.

"What the devil is going on?" Neither of them had heard Mr. Marks enter the room.

"The young master finished his letters, Sir, so I thought it best for 'im to be occupied with something. The devil makes work for idle 'ands as they say," Ellie answered. Harry shrank back, clearly trying to put as much distance as possible between himself and his tutor.

"Get out your history of the Kings and Queens of England," he barked at the child. He turned to Ella. "You are dismissed. You are to return tomorrow in the morning."

"Yes, Sir." She bobbed a curtsey, her hand on the door when she turned. "Could I take the young master into t'garden tomorrow if it's fine and if 'e's done his lessons, Sir? My young sisters always needed to run about before we could get them to do anything sensible."

"I shall consider it," he replied.

At least he did not say no. There was no doubt in her mind that Harry was the child the conspirators were planning to place on the throne and he was being schooled to ensure that he told the correct story to those who might doubt him. He seemed a bright, lively little boy when he was not in his tutor's presence. What they were doing was not only treason but cruelty to the boy and that she could not tolerate. The sooner he was rescued, the better; her own childhood told her all she needed to know about cruelty to children.

CHAPTER 23

For two weeks, Ella was summoned to attend to Harry in the tower; she was even permitted to take him into the grounds so long as they could be seen from the library windows, so any chance of spiriting him away was remote. Whenever she risked a glance at the windows there was always the shadow of someone standing watching them. However, Harry did seem to be more at ease in her presence, and she had been able to make him laugh once or twice when she told him of the antics of some of the animals she had rescued. There was no doubt that he was both unhappy and in danger.

"Absolutely not," Stephen said when she told him of her plan to rescue the boy. "I agree, he needs to be rescued as soon as possible, but we must wait until the conspirators are captured, otherwise it may alert them to the fact that there are those whom they consider to be traitors in their midst."

"Very well," Ella reluctantly agreed, "but at the latest we must rescue him the night of the masquerade, I dread to think what will happen to him. I fear if he is no longer of use there will be no incentive to keep him alive."

"Quite." Stephen paused. "I do not like the idea of the boy being held any more than you do, but I give you my word that he shall be rescued as soon as the masquerade ball begins."

"It is, I suppose, the best we can do," she conceded.

"Does the boy know why he is being held here?"

Ella nodded. "I think so, he told me he was not allowed to say, and he is terrified of Mr. Marks who is instructing him in the kings and queens of England, though bullying would be a better word."

"And is there any logical reason for this boy to have been chosen?" Stephen mused.

"He has bright red hair which I believe is a Tudor trait, he is I imagine from the area where the so-called son of Elizabeth was supposed to have been spirited away to, but beyond that it is my opinion that they approached the boy's parents with the promise of riches and they found it impossible to refuse."

"They did not just pick some random orphan from a foundling hospital then?"

She shook her head. "Harry talks with fondness of his mother and father."

Stephen also shook his head. "What monsters are we dealing with who would use an innocent child for their nefarious purposes?"

"They are people who will stop at nothing to get what they want," she replied.

He took her in his arms. "I cannot wait until this is all over and we may return to something resembling a normal life," he said before kissing her. "And now I must go, the masquerade is but days away and there is much to be done."

"There is something else," she whispered, not wanting the moment in his arms to end, but end it must. "I am concerned about the whereabouts of the earl. It is his castle after all and the invitations have gone out in his name, but there is no sign of him at the castle. You would think he would be there supervising things, but everyone seems to be at the beck and call of this Lord Oliver. Do you not think this is strange?"

Stephen stepped back. "Do you believe something has happened to him?"

"I could not say for sure, but I intend to find out. Barbara says..."

"Barbara says what?" he prompted.

"Barbara says she thinks there is someone else imprisoned in one of the other towers, she has seen a footman take food up there, but no-one else is to go near."

He placed a finger under her chin and raised her head. "Ella, please promise me you will not do anything to put yourself at further risk."

"Of course not," she assured him.

"That is not a promise."

She rolled her eyes. "I promise that I shall not do anything to put myself at further risk," she intoned.

"You really do not learn about the eye-rolling, do you?" he said quietly, "and I for one am glad of it." He kissed her until they were both breathless. "I cannot forget our journey here and how I wish to see you once again in my bed, so that I may make love to you from dusk to dawn and hear your voice as you cry my name." He uttered a deep sigh. "But now I really must go."

"The castle is almost prepared, and we are just awaiting the arrival of the guests," she replied, not wanting him to leave.

"My preparations are almost ready, though I shall not reveal them to you. The less you know the better so that if by chance anyone were to question you, you will have nothing to say."

Ella nodded. "I can see the sense in that. I doubt that there will be anything else to de-cipher, the next part of the plot will be face to face among the conspirators."

"Indeed. Keep safe my love, it will not be long now before things can return to some semblance of normality."

Ella stared at the low ceiling, unable to sleep, both her mind and body restless as she remembered not only Stephen's kisses but his words. What did he mean by semblance of normality? His normality was vastly different from the small life she led with her aunt. Would he return to his life of intrigue and danger? Would she just be a pleasant interlude he had enjoyed, a pleasant memory that would fade in time or a distraction from the pressures of the mission he had undertaken? Or was there a chance that there was a future for them? She wanted to believe that with all her heart, she wanted to awaken each morning with Stephen by her side, she wanted to talk with him, listen to him, she wanted to know what books he enjoyed, what his favourite foods were, what colour he liked and what he thought about religion, philosophy and politics, the mundane and the deep. He desired her as she desired him, that was in no doubt, but what did they have to build a future on? They had been somewhat thrown together by this mission, and it could well be that once it was over, the attraction would fade. He had once proposed to her out of pity, and she could not bear it if that was all he still felt for her, but surely now she had shown she was worthy of his respect, even though she doubted that he would ever love her. She turned over and thumped her pillow, she did not want that to be the case, because she knew in her heart that there would be no other man for her than Stephen.

"Well, there's definitely summat goin' on in that tower," Barbara said as they walked home. "I 'ad to take a tray up there because that footman is poorly. I got to the top o' t'stairs and I 'ate them spiral stairs, when this 'uge oaf of a man appears and says, 'I'll take that, now get on your way.' and off 'e goes, takes out a key and opens the door."

"Did he say anything to whoever is in the chamber?" Ella asked.

"I couldn't swear to it, but it sounded like, 'ere's yer dinner, milord."

"It is the earl, I am sure of it," Ella replied.

"What's goin' on?" Barbara asked. "That poor young lad in one tower and a gentleman in the other."

"I think it is all to do with the matter we are here to investigate. I think it means we shall have two people to rescue," Ella replied.

"Not sure the duke'll like that."

"He will deal with the matter, have no doubt on that score, but I think it also means we must be extra vigilant. We may be only humble maids in their eyes, but we now know about the man in the tower and the boy, they may decide that we already know too much," Ella said, glad that the darkness hid her expression from Barbara. She had not felt particularly worried until now.

There was the sound of shouting, weeping and the resounding crash of something thrown at the door as Ella approached the tower to watch over the young boy. As she entered, she could see Harry cowering against the bed as his tutor towered above him brandishing a stick. "You are the most miserably stupid boy I have ever had the misfortune to come across," he shouted, his face red with fury. "You are incapable of learning the simplest thing, how we are going to pass you off as..." his voice petered out as he became aware of Ella standing in the doorway.

"What do you want, girl?" he shouted.

"I've come to watch over the young master while you go to see 'is lordship," she replied, evenly, though every part of her wanted to wrest the stick from his hands and beat him with it. Her own father had not been averse to physical punishment but a look at Harry told her that this had been a severe beating, one eye was swollen and there was a bruise forming on his cheek.

"Very well," the tutor appeared to have calmed down, "but the boy is to have nothing to eat for the rest of the day, it might help him to focus on his learning." He swept out of the room.

Ella waited until she was sure Mr. Marks had reached the bottom of the staircase when she took hold of Harry's hand and pulled him upright. She quickly pulled his clothes out of the wooden chest at the end of the bed and tied them in a bundle.

"What are you doing?" the boy asked.

"We're leaving," she replied. "Come with me."

"But what about Mr. Marks? He'll beat me again."

She knelt down and put her hands on his shoulders. "Harry, I promise that I shall take you to a place where you are going to be safe and no-one will beat you. Now, do you want to come?"

The boy nodded.

"Good," she replied. "We are going down the steps and out of the tower, then we shall go down the servants' stairs and out through the kitchen garden. At the end of the garden there is a door which leads to a wood. Run through the wood to the village and knock on the door of the last house. The woman who lives there is called Mrs. Gamble, tell her I sent you and that she must hide you. We are going to have to move quickly, before anyone realises we are gone, do you think you can do that?"

He nodded again. She held out her hand. "Then come along."

She slipped back into the castle and up to the tower as fast as she could. By the time Mr. Marks re-appeared; she was unconscious, apparently having knocked her head on the chest, with a fine bruise appearing on her temple. He dragged her to her feet.

"What is the name of all that's holy is going on here?" he demanded. "And where is the boy?"

CHAPTER 24

"Tell me again what happened," Lord Oliver said, his voice quietly menacing.

"Like I said, my lord. We was playin' a chase game in the tower an' I must 'ave slipped and banged my 'ead. When I came round, Mr. Marks 'ere was standin' over me an' the boy 'ad gone," Ella said. "Do yer think 'e might 'ave gone down to the lake, 'e does like it there, 'e told me 'e likes to fish with 'is daddy?" she asked, hoping she was not over doing her role.

"The child is nowhere to be seen," Mr. Marks said, his voice tight with anger. "I have men searching the estate and there is no sign of him.

"Yer don't think 'e could 'ave fallen in?" Ella asked, wiping her face with her apron, "I don't think the little man can swim." If she could concentrate on Harry possibly being in the lake, they may take less notice of her own role in his disappearance. "Should I go and look for 'im, 'e knows me, if 'e's 'iding, 'e might come out for me. 'E might me afeared to if 'e thinks 'e's in trouble."

"The boy is most certainly in trouble," Lord Oliver replied, "however, you will remain here under lock and key. I have not finished with you."

Mr. Marks strode over to her and stared into her eyes. "There is something about you, girl, I cannot put my finger on it, but should we find that you are involved in any way with the boy's disappearance, you will rue the day you were born."

She returned his stare with what she hoped looked like innocent indignation. "I didn't 'ave nothin' to do with it, yer 'onour."

He grasped her chin, forcing her head back. "I don't believe you. That child was a meek and snivelling brat until you were sent to look after him. He would never have either thought of or had the courage to even attempt to leave the tower on his own. Lord Oliver may be convinced by your tale, but I am not, and there are ways of getting the truth out of you and I shall be only too pleased to use them. Think about that, Miss." He turned on his heel and strode from the room. The lock clicked shut behind him.

There was nothing for it, she was going to have to escape, but how? He had locked the door, but she had no doubt that one of the servants would be posted outside, similarly, the grounds were swarming with footmen searching for Harry, who, she hoped by now was hidden in Mrs. Gamble's loft. She looked around and suddenly remembered the priest hole. She had only been a child when she had been brought here by her aunt, possibly when the current earl's grandfather was alive. Peter, the current earl who was a few years older than her, had thought it a great jest to put her in the priest hole which had been there since Tudor times when being Catholic was a crime and many priests were protected and hidden by powerful families who were not willing to convert to the new Protestant religion. The family would take in the priest who would celebrate the illegal mass and if soldiers arrived to search the house, the priest would be hidden until they had gone. If a priest was found it did not go well, the family would, at the very least have their lands, titles and possessions confiscated and even lose their heads, it never went well for the priest. Eventually though in the case of the Bolton's, self-preservation meant that they changed, but the priest hole remained. It was behind the oak panelling which, as far as she could see, had not been affected by the renovations.

The lever to open the hiding place was somewhere in the intricate carving of the fireplace. In the centre was a coat of arms with two lions rampant and a knight's shield, and what looked like rambling thorns surrounding the whole thing, but nothing resembling any kind of lever. She stepped back and took a breath. "Come on, Ella, this is what you do, look for symbols. Look again." Then she saw in, in the middle of the shield was a Tudor rose, the red of the House of Lancaster entwined with the white rose of the House of York. "That is it," she said, pressing the rose in the centre. For a second, nothing happened, then the three panels to the right of the fire-place creaked and slid open. Ella looked around in case someone had heard but the door to the library remained firmly closed. Before she entered the room, she quickly went to one of the large windows and opened it, hoping that whoever discovered that she had escaped would assume that she had gone through there and would not look for her in the castle.

Ella stepped into the small space behind the panel and pressed the lever to her right and breathed a sigh of relief when the panel swung shut behind her. It was a small space, and she had to remind herself to breathe slowly, she had never been comfortable in small spaces since Peter had shoved her in there as a child, nor did she like the lack of light but had she remained in the library she had a feeling that things would not go well. Mercifully, there was a seat which she sank onto.

It could have been minutes, or it could have been hours, the blackness and silence made the passing of time difficult to judge, but she was suddenly aware that someone had entered the library. She leaned towards the panelling.

"What the devil? Marks," the voice she recognised as Lord Oliver bellowed. "Marks, get in here."

"Where the devil is the girl, I thought I told you to ensure she stayed in here."

"She was in here when I left, I locked the door."

"You fool, first the boy and now the chit. People do not just disappear."

There were footsteps and scuffling as though they were searching the room. "The damn window is open, so she must have gone out that way and escaped through the gardens."

"Impossible, there are ten men out there already looking for the boy, she would have been seen, and why the hell did you not ensure the windows were locked."

There was a pause before Mr. Marks responded. "She's a sly bitch, I don't believe she was a real maid, she was too cocky, too sure of herself. I never felt she showed the proper respect. She was also curious about the boy; it would not surprise me if she hadn't persuaded the truth out of him."

"The lack of respect matters not, the fact is that she knows about the boy, we need that boy back."

"And the maid?"

"She will need to be disposed of; we are close to achieving our aim and I refuse to tolerate the idea that our plans may be scuppered by one stupid female with loose lips and a foolish boy. They cannot have gone far, tell the men to widen the search."

Ella heard one set of footsteps receding and the door slammed. She almost jumped out of her skin when a quiet voice said, "Where are you, Ella Grainger? I will find you and I will kill you." Lord Oliver must have been standing right in front of the panelling.

There was no way of knowing whether it was day or night, she was cramped and stiff in the priest hole, but Ella dared not venture out until she was sure there was no-one still in the library. Lord Oliver's quiet voice had scared her. It was one thing for him to suspect that she was not the maid but quite another for him to actually know who she was. And if he knew about her, what else did he know? Did he have a suspicion that their plans had been infiltrated and worse, was Stephen walking into some kind of ambush. She could not sit and wait; she would have to warn him.

Suddenly, she became aware of a thin line of light below the panelling. Someone had entered the room with a candle, so now she knew it was dark. There was a chink of glass as someone poured themselves a drink.

"Ah, you had better have news and it had better be good," Lord Oliver spoke.

"There is no sight nor sound of either of them," Mr. Marks replied. "I even went to every house in the village, and no-one has seen anything. They could be hiding in the woods, but the men have been searching all day. They can search again in the morning, and we can use the hounds in the woods. They cannot have gone far. We will find them."

"Make sure we do. I cannot allow anything to distract us from our task. I have no doubt that all those who are attending the masquerade will join us but we must have the boy. The so-called maid we shall deal with later."

"So-called maid?"

"Never mind, it is the boy who must be found."

"I have to say that the boy is something of a disappointment, mayhap we should have found one with a better grasp of learning." Mr. Marks mused.

"No, we need a boy who understands little of the enormity of what we are about to do."

"And what happens when the boy becomes of age, the inner council may act as regent, but will both he and the people expect him to assume a greater role in kingship when he reaches his majority? Or will that be the moment when we declare the republic?" Even through the panelling, Ella could hear the excitement in Mr. Marks' voice.

Ella leaned closer to the panelling and held her breath, "I have been considering the matter deeply, and I have decided that, when the time comes, I shall declare myself king."

"King?" the word bounced around the room.

"The populace will be used to seeing me as leader, the boy, as you rightly surmise, is not fitted for the responsibility of high office and that will become more apparent as he grows. He is weak intellectually as a boy and will be a weak king, which will be acceptable when he is a boy, but a disaster when he is a man. No, he will have an accident or catch some disease that will carry him off before he reaches manhood."

"But that is not what this whole enterprise is about, we were in agreement to rid our country of the House of Hanover and replace it with a republic, so that the people of England would be free of the aristocracy, and that the common man should have greater power, that wealth should be divided equally and a man's position in society should not be determined by the bed he was born in." Ella could hear the passion and fury in Mr. Marks' words.

"My dear Marks, do you really think that the common man is either capable or worthy of taking on greater power and wealth? He would not have the slightest idea of what to do with it and probably never will. The common people are like children. They need to be treated firmly with just enough distraction to keep them happy with their lot. Once they have played their part in the uprising, they will go back to their small lives and continue living as they have for centuries, serving their masters."

"That is not the agreement. I have not risked my life for this."

There was another pause. "We all have our roles to play in this small revolution, though now, I fear, your role is over, Marks."

There was a thud and the candle was snuffed out.

CHAPTER 25

Although she had no idea of time, Ella had not heard a sound in the room for what felt like hours, she could not stay hidden behind the panelling forever and she needed to ensure both that Harry was safe and that Stephen knew what she had overheard. She tentatively pressed the lever and waited for the mechanism to begin, she held her breath, it sounded so loud she was sure that the whole castle could hear, but as the panel swung open, no-one had apparently heard, she stepped cautiously into the room, closing the pane behind her. It was indeed dark; the only light was the full moon coming in through the windows.

She stifled a scream as she saw the apparently lifeless body of Marks in front of the desk, he was face down but even in the dim light she could see a pool of blood on the carpet beneath him. If he was dead then the only person who could have done the deed was Lord Oliver, and somehow, he knew who she was, furthermore, she had no doubt of her own fate if he found her, he had said so himself. Knowing that she could be discovered at any moment and also knowing that there was little if nothing she could do for Marks, she slid the window open as silently as she could and climbed out. She could not risk going across the lawn where she might easily be seen in the moonlight, she kept close to the house until she reached the kitchen garden then dashed to the shadow of the wall. The door to the estate was unlocked and she slipped through before running for the shelter of the woods. The crunch of her feet on the gravel path and the breaking of twigs felt loud enough to awaken the dead but she dared not stop until she reached the back lane leading to the village.

Fortunately, there was a candle still burning in the window of Mrs. Gamble's cottage, so she paused to catch her breath then tentatively lifted the latch and went inside. No-one in the village locked their doors at night, no-one had anything to steal, though she was afraid that somehow, Lord Oliver had made the connection between them, on the other hand, she reasoned, he no doubt thought that the living arrangements of the servants was beneath him.

"Oh, thank the Lord you're 'ere." Never had Ella been so thankful to hear a familiar voice and before she could reply, she was enveloped in Barbara's arms. "Sorry my lady, if that was too familiar, but I was so worried when yer didn't come 'ome. Mrs. 'eaton said you'd been delayed looking for the little lad, but I knew that was a lie 'cause the little lad was 'ere."

Ella sank down on the settle in exhaustion and relief. "Harry is here?"

Barbara shook her head. "Not now. We sent a message to the duke, and he sent men to come and take 'im to safety."

"Thank God," Ella replied, and suddenly could not stop herself from shaking.

"It's the shock," Barbara said, "'ere." She held out a cup of tea. "I'd just made meself a cup, Mrs Gamble keeps a goodly tea caddy that's for sure, strong an' sweet, that's what yer need."

Ella nodded and took a sip, and wrinkled her nose. Although the fashion was for sugar in tea, it was not a taste she enjoyed, but for the moment she appreciated its soothing quality. "Is Harry all right?" she asked. "I had to get him away from there. Is the duke furious?"

"Well," Barbara put her hands on her hips. "'e ain't best pleased that's for sure, but e'll no doubt tell yer 'imself, 'e said e'd be back when e'd taken care of t'boy. If yer want my opinion, 'e were worried about yer. Now yer should get to bed, yer looks done in."

Ella shook her head. "No, you go on up, I will sit here for a little while in case the duke returns. I could not possibly sleep now in any case."

"Very well my lady, but if yer needs anythin', just call." Barbara lit another candle and made her way to the small door leading to the stairs. "I don't know what's goin' on at yon castle, but it's not safe for yer or anybody else if yer ask me," she said as she left the room.

Contrary to her words, the minute Barbara had left the room an overwhelming sense of weariness overtook her, and Ella lay down on the settle and surrendered to sleep. It was the slightest noise, but she was instantly awake, someone was in the room, someone who was trying to be quiet. As her eyes adjusted to the dim light, she grabbed the first thing that came to hand to defend herself with.

"What were you planning to do with that?" Stephen's amused voice cut through her fear. "Beat me to a pulp and make an omelette?"

"Stephen, oh thank goodness you're here," she cried, dropping the frying pan and stepping into his open arms. The tears that she had kept back since her interrogation at the castle, started to fall and she could not seem to stop. "It was horrible," she sobbed, "Lord Oliver knows who I am and he killed Mr. Marks. He only wants Harry for a little while, then he is going to kill him and declare himself king."

Stephen held her, trying to soothe her, stroking her back and hair, whispering, "It is over, Ella, you are safe now, I have you."

She raised tear filled eyes towards him. "I do not think anyone is safe. Lord Oliver is a madman who will, I fear, stop at nothing."

"Ella, I will need to hear all of this, but first I need to get you to safety."

"What of Barbara and Mrs. Gamble?"

"They will tell the truth that they have not seen you and thought you were still at the castle, looking for the lad, which is what Barbara was told. There is no reason for anyone to suspect that they know more, no-one is aware of your connection with Mrs. Gamble except the housekeeper and she is trustworthy. Here." He wrapped a thick cloak around her. "We must leave now and you cannot take anything with you, that way it looks as though you are coming back." He saw a shawl lying on the settle. "Is this yours?" She nodded. He scooped it up and placed it in his jacket. "It may well be of use," was all he said by way of explanation.

"Where are we going?"

"To Wensley, and we shall make further plans when we are there."

The journey was slower than he would have liked, but with Ella riding in front of him he could not push his horse to go faster. His relief at finding her fast asleep on the settle was unlike any feeling he had ever experienced. He knew she was in danger when he received the message that the young boy was hidden in Mrs. Gamble's loft, they would naturally believe that Ella had something to do with his escape as she had been the last one to see him and the child had not been allowed out of the tower before. He frowned, the fact that Lord Oliver knew that she was Lady Ella Grainger troubled him more, how would they have found that out? He had men situated in the castle in preparation for the interception of the conspirators, could one of them be a turncoat? From what he had learned of this Lord Oliver, he would stop at nothing to get at Ella, especially if he suspected her of disrupting his plans. He tightened his arms on the woman in front of him, he did not know how he would live if anything happened to her but he would protect her, with his own life if necessary. Life without her would be at best half a life, they had sparred and fought and she had demanded to be part of this mission, but he knew, even if she did not, that they were meant to be together, and he would prove it to her. As the horse stepped onto Carter's bridge, he removed the shawl from his jacket and flung it into the river. It might be enough to convince Lord Oliver that Ella had escaped but had drowned in the river.

He was relieved when the house came into view, at least at Wensley Ella would be safe. He quickly dismounted and lifted her down.

"What are you doing?" she said, sleepily.

"I am carrying you into the house," he replied, "and there is to be no argument, you are exhausted." He climbed the stairs and kicked open the door to the duchess' bedroom where a maid was tending to the fire. "Help her ladyship to bed," he said, gently laying Ella down on the bed and dropping a kiss on her forehead. "Sleep now, my love, I shall see you in the morning."

Although he felt relief that Ella was now safe, sleep eluded him. He heard the hall clock strike three and then became aware of another sound. At first, he thought it was some sort of animal, a fox perhaps in the grounds. He sat up, the sound was coming from Ella's room. He leapt out of bed, threw open the connecting door, and saw the bed was empty. Glancing around the room, his heart beating like a drum, he suddenly saw her, huddled in the corner, almost covered by the long drapes.

"Ella, I am here," he said, softly walking slowly towards her.

"No," she cried. "You must not come closer. Stay away. Stay behind me, Harry, I will try to keep you safe."

Stephen frowned. He could see that although her eyes were open, she could not see him. "Stay in here with me. It is very small, and they will not see you in here, but you must be quiet," she continued.

"Ella," he said quietly, "it is all right. You are safe here."

She turned to look at him, and he began to think that she was coming back to the present, "And Harry? Is he safe?"

"Harry is safe," he confirmed. "He is on his way to another of my estates in the care of men who will protect him."

"Thank you. I feel I must apologise."

"For what?" He hunkered down beside her. She picked at the lace on her nightrail. "My impulsive action in getting Harry to run away may have put the whole mission in danger," she said. "But I could not stand by and let him be beaten any more. Mr. Marks was nothing more than a brute and seemed to take pleasure in inflicting pain on the boy."

"I saw the bruises and weals on his back, schoolmasters are often handy with their canes and sometimes get the prefects to do it for them, but the injuries inflicted by Marks were beyond anything I have ever seen. You did the right thing and, bear in mind, although it might cause us to refine our plans, it will also cause problems for the traitors who will not be able to produce the child who would be king."

She dropped her head and hugged her knees. "I feel so weak and foolish," she admitted. "But I have had a fear of small, dark spaces ever since I was a child. It started when Peter thought it would be a great jest to shut me in the priest hole, but my father used to lock me in the cellars when I was bad, or just so that he did not have to look at me. I always feared that he would forget about me, and I believe that is what he wanted to do."

He took both her hands in his. "Ella, believe me, you are neither weak nor foolish. I can think of no other woman who would have had the courage, strength and intellect to both get Harry out of there and find the hiding place, and stay in that dark, cold space for hours, let alone escape knowing that you could have been discovered at any time, not to mention stepping over a dead body. Most women would have either swooned or had an attack of the vapours and many men too. You are, however..."

She looked up at him. "Frozen, let's get you into bed before you turn into a lump of ice."

He raised her hands to his lips before helping her to stand.

"Would you stay with me tonight? Please?" she asked. "I don't want to be alone tonight."

"Of course." He nodded. "I shall be happy to serve as your warming pan." *If that is all I can be then so be it, I shall be content with holding you in my arms, I shall have to be.*

CHAPTER 26

"Tell me," Stephen said softly, "tell me what you want Ella, and I will give it to you." His eyes gleamed like molten silver in the moonlight coming through the open window. They were both naked, their clothes in a tangle on the floor. He took her hand and placed it on his chest. "Do you feel my heart-beat? It beats faster because of you." His large hand covered hers and moved it slowly down his abdomen and closed it over his erect member. "This," he murmured against her ear, causing tingles to travel down to her very core, "this is what you do to me, and now I am going to have you Ella, in ways you cannot even imagine. I am going to give you the greatest pleasure a man can give a woman, but you must tell me what it is you want."

"I want," she murmured, "I want..."

"What? What do you want?"

Ella's eyes snapped open. It was true, she was in bed with Stephen, neither of them was naked, but her face coloured as she imagined that Stephen could, somehow, see into her dream. "Nothing," she muttered, turning away from him so he could not see her face, "it was just a dream."

She could feel him behind her. "It sounds like a very interesting dream from the tone of your voice and the way you were thrashing about. I am particularly interested to know what it is that you want," he said with amusement clear in his voice.

"Is that what I said? I don't remember," she lied.

He turned her to face him. "Oh, I think you do," he replied. "Well, if you truly cannot remember, perhaps we should try and jog your memory. Was it perhaps this?" His hand cupped the back of her head as he lowered his lips and caught her mouth in a stunning kiss. "Or perhaps this?" His eyes gleamed as his other hand found her breast through the thin material of her nightrail. "Hmmm," he said, lightly rubbing her nipple, "I rather think you like that, is that what you want?"

"Stephen," she sighed. Ripples of pleasure were beginning to course through her body.

"I think we can dispense with this," Stephen said, pulling her nightrail over her head so that she was naked. "Now my lady, you are a feast for my eyes, a cornucopia of loveliness."

Ella rolled her eyes.

"Tut, tut my lady, you still have not learned your lesson regarding the eye rolling," he said softly, lowering his head and taking one nipple into his mouth, sucking and gently biting it whilst attending to the other with his fingers, causing Ella to gasp. "Or perhaps this is what you want, Ella." Even his breath caused shivers down her spine as he kissed his way down her navel towards the neat tangle of curls. He dipped his head and ran his tongue along her core. "I think I am getting closer to what you want, am I not?"

She cried out and gripped the sheets as his tongue dipped inside her. Ella's eyes flew open as wave after wave of sensation washed over her entire body and Stephen continued relentlessly until she stilled, then he moved so that her head was once again resting on his chest and he lazily stroked her hair.

"You seem to know what I want without my needing to

explain it," she whispered. "But what of you? What is it that you want?" she asked.

"I want to have you, Ella, not only in my bed, but I can assure you that I definitely want you there, or on the desk in my study, on the dining table, on the sofa, against the books in the library and anywhere else I can make love to you. But it is not just about bedsport, I want you by my side, at the theatre, as we sit and read books together, as we ride, as we dine, as we sleep. There is a connection between us Ella, there always has been even though you have tried to deny it. We have wasted too much time, and I want to strengthen those bonds between us. I want the opportunity to love and protect you. I want to ask..."

She put her hand gently over his mouth. "Whatever you are going to ask, Stephen, please save it until our mission is completed. Nothing is normal now, our emotions are heightened and we may both say things that in the cold light of day, we regret. Let us wait until we return to normality before we make hasty decisions."

"Very well," he conceded. "But my feelings on this matter are constant, I want you to know that. And now," his hands traced a light pattern down her side, "now it is time to attend further to your wants." He rolled her onto her back as his fingers found her core. "You are more than ready," he said softly. "Just say the words, Ella, and your wants shall be satisfied."

She looked into his eyes. "I want you inside me, Stephen. I want to feel you move against me. I want you to make love to me."

"Then who am I to refuse?"

She sighed as he entered her and moved with him as his thrusts became harder and faster. "Oh," she cried as her body pulsed with pleasure.

It took all of Stephen's control to pull out before his own climax, he wanted nothing more than to come inside her, but he would not, they were taking enough risks as it was.

"Why do you do that?" she asked, when they had both regained their breath?

"I told you, I cannot and will not risk the chance of getting you with child. You would be completely ruined, and Elliott would have my head."

"I do not think that the ton would be remotely interested in the life of a spinster, I think I am rather too old to be ruined," she replied. The prospect of motherhood had always seemed to be beyond reach and, when she was younger, she had resigned herself to the thought that it would never happen, that she was destined to become an old maid. But now she thought of it, there was a deep pull in both body and mind to have a child to love.

"You know as well as I do," his voice interrupted her thoughts, "that the ton is both fickle and cruel and a salacious scandal of an earl's daughter bearing a child without a wedding ring is guaranteed to get tongues wagging. They would cut you to ribbons. I will not have that."

"You are too honourable, Stephen," she acknowledged. "I am not sure that I agree with you, but many men would not care."

"How often do I have to tell you that I am not many men? Sleep now my sweet, we have much to do in the morning." Although she had obeyed Stephen's command to sleep, he reached for her twice more in the night, each time bringing her to a shattering climax before they slept again.

As the first fingers of daylight were reaching through the curtains, Ella woke up with a start. There was a dent in the pillow where Stephen's head had been, but the bed was cold, indicating that he had left some time ago. She rose, washed and dressed quickly and found him in the library bending over the desk studying a document. "There you are," she said, trying to keep any accusation out of her voice. "I wondered where you were."

He came towards her and drew her into his arms for a lingering kiss. "You were sleeping so peacefully I did not want to wake you. Come, let us break our fast and then perhaps a ride?"

She smiled. "That would be most acceptable, but what of the plans for the Masquerade? It is only days away. I have been thinking...."

"As ever," he interrupted her, "but first things first and the most important first thing is breakfast." He drew her arm through his and walked towards the breakfast room.

"Now," Ella began, when she had eaten the eggs and bacon that Stephen had loaded her plate with. "I have been thinking about the Masquerade, and I think it would be best if I attend as your young male cousin or such. Dressed as a boy of course."

Stephen spluttered as the drink of coffee he had taken caught in his throat. "Dressed as a boy? In breeches?"

"Naturally in breeches since a boy is unlikely to be wearing a dress," she replied, with a grin. "Far more sensible and if there is to be any fighting, much better for speed and movement."

Stephen leaned forwards, his elbows on the table and templed his fingers. "Firstly, if, or rather when there is to be any fighting, I do not want you to be anywhere near it. Secondly, this Lord Oliver, whoever he is, is quite likely to recognise you and that might give the whole game away before we get to the rest of the leadership. So you will not be attending the masquerade at all, Ella."

She scowled. "That is ridiculous. I know those tunnels and I know where the earl is being kept. I know the ins and outs of the castle better than anyone, as a maid I learned the ways used by both the nobles and the shortcuts and backstairs used by the servants. Besides which, I can ride as well as any man, shoot a pistol accurately and wield a rapier, quite apart from the hand to hand combat I have already demonstrated. Frankly, you would be a fool not to take me."

"Need I remind you how recently you had to hide in the priest hole and witness the murder in cold blood of the tutor? Not to mention the nightmares this caused you."

"I was weak, I am not usually so," she shot back. "I am quite recovered and if anyone deserves the chance to bring Lord Oliver to justice, surely it is I."

He took both her hands in his. "Ella, you are the strongest woman I have ever known, be in no doubt about that, but can you not see that I do not want to place you in any situation where you will be in danger. This Lord Oliver, and I seriously doubt that is his name, is dangerous and unpredictable. We know he is not averse to killing in cold blood. Personally, I believe the man to be deranged, and I will need you to bear witness to what you heard and saw when you were working there."

She took a deep breath, expelling it slowly. "I want to know how Lord Oliver knows who I am and why he wants to kill me. There was something about the way he said it, as though I have mortally offended him in some way, but as far as I know, I had never met the man until I went to work at the castle."

"All the more reason why you should stay here in safety."

"All the more reason why I need to go and see this through." She took a breath. "Before you agreed to me coming on this mission, you said things which led me to believe that you understood about the small lives women are forced, because of their gender, to live. I need to do this, not just for myself, Stephen, but for all women, so that powerful men like you will see for yourselves, that we can be so much more than the role demanded of ladies, as is shown, I might add, by the tasks done by women of lower classes who are not treated as though they are hothouse flowers."

He gazed into her eyes for a long moment. "Very well." He sighed. "I have been persuaded by your logic and powerful arguments, please do not make a habit of that."

She smiled at him, before drawing him in for a kiss. "Now let us take that ride, and then, duke, I shall take you to my bedchamber and have my wicked way with you."

"Dear God, woman, you are going to kill me, one way or the other."

CHAPTER 27

During the next few days, more men began to arrive as the date for the mission grew nearer.

"I doubt many of you know Lady Ella Grainger," Stephen said, addressing the twelve men gathered in the library, "but she has already played a vital part in this mission and will be joining us when we complete it."

"Are you insane, Hart? This mission is no place for a woman," a red faced, older man who had been introduced as Sir Montague Shoreham, spluttered.

"I can assure you that were it not for Lady Ella, none of us would be here. We should not even know of the plot, let alone know the details of where and who the conspirators are. It was Lady Ella who was able to decipher the enigma when none of our best men could. It was also Lady Ella who infiltrated Bolton Castle, at significant danger to herself I might add, and discovered the young boy who was supposed to pass as the rightful heir to the English throne, as well as this Lord Oliver who appears to be the mastermind behind the plot."

"That is all very well, Hart, but in the heat of combat, we cannot afford a weak link," Sir Montague persisted.

"Let me assure you, Lady Ella is anything but a weak link," Stephen countered.

"I rather think that an exhibition might settle the issue," Ella spoke for the first time.

"Outrageous, a gentleman does not attack a woman," Sir Montague shot back amid a quiet chorus of agreement from some of the others.

"Are you afraid of being bested by a woman, Sir?" Ella replied.

"Of course not, everyone knows that women are the gentler sex, it would be most unfair."

Ella looked around the room. "I shall go and ready myself, and when I return, I challenge whoever you have decided to pit me against. If your man wins, then I shall retire and we shall say no more about the matter, but if I beat him, then I shall join the mission and there will be no more carping and complaining. Does that sound agreeable?"

There was a confident murmur of assent as she left the room.

When she returned ten minutes later, she was clad in form fitting breeches and a shirt with a small dagger in her boot. She had tied her hair back so that her opponent would not have the advantage of grasping it. The centre of the room had been cleared of furniture and a man of about thirty stood to one side, his hip resting against the edge of the desk, looking bored.

"This is Lord Willoughby, one of our experienced men," Stephen said, with a gleam in his eye, knowing that Willoughby and the others were in for something of a surprise. Ella nodded. Without further ado, Willoughby charged towards her, one arm outstretched, clearly his intention was to grasp her around the throat. Within seconds he was on his back with his arm twisted behind him. There was a moment of silence before the room erupted in a buzz of conversation.

"My God, did you see that?"

"She had him at her mercy with the ease of taking sweetmeats from a child."

"I have never seen the like, from man or woman."

"I have heard of female warriors in the jungles of South America, but I should never have imagined that I should see one here, in a library in England."

"Is it some kind of enchantment do you think?"

Ella could not help but smile. "Really, Lord Willoughby, surely you know better than to signal to your opponent your intentions," she said quietly, "and please do not attempt to struggle or your arm will come out of its socket, and you will be of little use on this mission." She sat back and released him.

"Extraordinary," Sir Montague said.

"As I told you, Lady Ella is more than capable of defending herself in close combat," Stephen said, the pride in his voice evident.

"But what about a weapon, what if her opponent has a dagger for example?" Sir Montague asked.

"I am here, Sir, and quite capable of answering for myself," she shot back. "Here," she said, drawing the knife from her boot and tossing it to Lord Willoughby. "This time, I shall turn my back so that there is an element of surprise. And Lord Willoughby, please do not seek to make it easy for me on account of my being a woman, as I suspect you did last time."

"Attacking an unarmed woman at all, let alone from behind, is not the behaviour of a gentleman," Sir Montague blustered.

"Really, Sir Montague, do you think those involved in this plot to kill the king and usurp his throne are likely to adhere to the niceties of gentlemanly behaviour?" Ella replied. "Now, Lord Willoughby, if you please." She turned her back.

The silence that descended on the room was in fact a help to Ella as she could hear Willoughby's approach from his breathing as he drew closer. She whipped around and instead of trying to knock the knife from his hand, closed on his bicep and pinched which caused him to yelp and drop the knife. Then she quickly took his legs from under him and with his good arm held tightly behind his back, retrieved the knife and held it to his throat.

"Of course," she explained, "with a real enemy, the knife would not remain unused." She tucked it back in her boot. "Now gentlemen, is there any other exhibition of my skills that you would care to see? I can hit a target accurately with a pistol and have some experience with a rapier. However, I should mention that I have no training with bow and arrow or poison." She held her hand out to assist Lord Willoughby up.

Without warning, Willoughby grasped her hand and instead of being helped up, he yanked her down and straddled her, his hands around her throat. "I will not be bested by a woman," he ground out. Instead of trying to free the hands around her throat, Ella's thumbs instantly reached for his eyes and pressed. "If I press for ten more seconds Willoughby, your eyes will pop out and it will take you longer than that to squeeze the life out of me," she could only whisper.

"What the hell?" Stephen roared, reaching for the young man, just as he fell back screaming and pawing at his eyes. "You bitch," he shouted. "I cannot see."

"Your sight will return, I did not apply sufficient pressure to ensure lasting damage," Ella replied calmly.

He turned to the others in the room, his face white with fury. "If you believe you will win this battle with the help of this she-devil, you are mistaken. There are many who will rally to our cause, they only await the call. You think Lord Oliver does not know what you are planning? You fools, he knows all and, as we speak, he is preparing. Your cause is lost and none of you will survive, including this treacherous bitch."

Further words were stopped as Stephen knocked him to the ground. "Take him to the cellar and bind him thoroughly," he ordered as two men began to drag the unconscious lord from the room. "We shall interrogate him later," he turned to Ella. "Are you all right?"

She nodded, rubbing her throat. "I believe there will be some bruising, but he did not have a chance to do any severe damage."

"But it was not for the want of trying," Stephen replied bitterly, wanting desperately to take her in his arms, but knowing that she would not want to appear weak in front of the other men. "I should say," she went on, "that the more important question now is whether Willoughby is working on his own, or whether there are other traitors."

Stephen turned to Sir Montague. "You introduced him Montague, how did you come to know him?"

"I knew his father, a good man who was loyal to our cause. Now that I think about it, he approached me. I suppose I just assumed that young Willoughby was as sound as his father," he finished quietly. "I apologise, Hart, it would seem I have put the entire mission in jeopardy."

"I doubt that," Stephen replied, his eyes narrowing. "Willoughby has not long been a member of our ranks and has not been party to any of our sensitive plans. What he may know, however, is the identity of this mysterious Lord Oliver who nobody seems to have knowledge of."

"Then we must interrogate him without delay," Sir Montague said.

"Warburton and Jennings, go and talk to him, see if you can get information about Lord Oliver, but do not use force, men are likely to say anything when tortured and little of it will be of use. Perhaps you may pretend to have sympathy with his views, in that way he may be lulled into a false sense of security and reveal more." The two men nodded and quickly left the room.

"And now gentlemen, to business." He pulled a chart from the drawer and laid it on the desk. "Lady Ella has been kind enough to provide us with a plan of the castle. The event will be held in the large chamber, the entrance for which is via the tunnel underneath the castle chapel. There is, however, a little used tunnel which can be used, for which the entrance is underneath the escarpment beneath the chapel and a third tunnel which may be accessed from the village church. I suggest we attack from both directions."

"And these tunnels, how do we access them without those at the castle knowing?"

"They were dug in the days when castles were besieged," Ella explained, "so that supplies may be got in and the occupants of the castle might escape if necessary. I played in these tunnels once or twice as a child and remember where the entrances are, though with the passing of years, I cannot guarantee that they are in a good state of repair."

"We shall have to deal with whatever we find, but we shall have the benefit of surprise on our side. How many men are we expecting to encounter?" one older man asked.

"Twenty at most. Many of the conspirators will be arrested on the road to the event, we will not take them sooner to ensure that they are unable to get a message to alert Lord Oliver. The ones who will be in attendance will no doubt be his most trusted allies."

"Are you sure he is still intent on proceeding, now that he has lost the boy?" another man asked.

"He will find another boy to suit his purposes, possibly one who cannot speak so that he can parade him about without suspicion, so long as he has red hair, that seemed to be the most important feature. In fact, a child who does not speak will suit his purposes better," Ella replied, thinking of the difficulty Harry had in learning his supposed ancestry. "It was quite clear to me that this man will stop at nothing until he has had his revolution and replaced parliament and the king with himself."

"And what of the earl? He must be in this up to his neck," Sir Montague spoke.

Ella shook her head. "I do not think so, in fact the earl is being kept prisoner in his own castle. I do not believe he is aware of what is going on and even if he is, there is nothing he can do to stop it."

"Then, gentlemen, it is up to us to see that this so-called revolution does not take place." He turned to Ella, adding, "and of course this most skilful and courageous lady." He bowed. "My lady, the king and the country are most grateful to you."

CHAPTER 28

That night their lovemaking was wilder than it had ever been, Stephen reached for her three times, each time playing her body as a maestro, bringing her to a shattering climax before he would take his own pleasure.

"I almost died when you told Willoughby to come at you with a knife," he admitted, tucking her against his side. "If something had happened..."

"Oh, ye of little faith," she said, poking him. "I was confident it would not. Willoughby is all show and bluster and, he has previously no doubt succeeded because of his size. He has never had to think of strategy, merely rush at his opponent like a bull at a gate, and being bested by a woman half his size did not sit well with him."

"And it was his frustration that led him to admit his treachery, and you are a third of his size."

"Did your men find out what he knows?" she asked.

Stephen shook his head. "He knows nothing. Apparently, he has never met with Lord Oliver, his only order came in the form of a letter, telling him to wheedle his way into government service. He knew Sir Montague had been a friend to his father and approached him. Montague took pity on him as, apparently, he was something of a loose cannon as a young man and came within a whisker of being disinherited. But Montague thought that a spell with some responsibility would be the making of him."

"Let me guess, when he came into his inheritance, he found there was nothing left, the estates were perhaps mortgaged to the hilt, and the family coffers were empty. Lord Oliver no doubt offered to restore his fortunes for a little information. Do I have the right of it?"

"More or less verbatim. How could you possibly know?"

"His boots and clothes were shabby, and he struck me as something of a vain man as well as a foolish one," she replied. "He would be of little use to Lord Oliver once the revolution was successful and I imagine, would be dealt with in the same way as Mr. Marks."

"I have a feeling that you are correct," he kissed the top of her head, "as you so often are."

"What will happen to him?"

"He will be taken to London and tried with the other conspirators we have captured."

Ella raised her head. "Other conspirators you have already captured?"

Stephen nodded. "With the list you found in the secret compartment in the desk, I decided to ensure the odds are on our side when we enter the tunnels. Oliver or whoever he is will be expecting around thirty men to attend his treasonous meeting and indeed, thirty have set off. However, fifteen were successfully intercepted a few miles from where they set off. They are all in custody in various parts of the country, all held separately so that they do not know of each other's incarceration, and none has been able to send a message to Oliver to cause any alarm."

"It is still possible though that someone may have alerted him

I suppose, perhaps one of the men's retinue may have slipped away unnoticed in the heat of the attack," she mused.

"Of course, but rest assured, we shall be prepared for whatever faces us."

She gave him a confident smile. "I should expect nothing less. Who are the ones we are expecting?"

"Mostly those who are within a three-day ride or less of the castle, but there are also one or two of the higher echelons of the ton who have falsely sworn allegiance to the king and whose names will come as quite a shock."

"A shock when the news of this revolt gets out?

He shook his head. "This news will never get out, it must remain secret, the country has not long been united, news of this revolt could embolden others to attempt the same and that would plunge the country once more into chaos as happened in France. It will be the king who is shocked by the treachery of men he thought were loyal to him."

"I wish we knew the identity, the real identity of Lord Oliver," she said.

"We shall find that out when we confront him," he assured her. "Now my love, try to rest, we shall need to be fresh for the final preparations, we ride to Bolton in two days time."

Two days passed very quickly, men arrived in small groups and were each given their orders. Following Ella's explanation of the layout of the castle of the leaders in the library, she was asked by Sir Montague to give the same information to the commanders of the groups. None of the men apparently found it remotely troubling that they were listening to a woman, she smiled at the thought. She was also asked to show the men the basics of the unarmed fighting technique she had exhibited.

"It is a pity I do not have more time to teach the men these moves," she said to Sir Montague, offering a hand to help him up from where she had deposited him on his generous rump.

"Indeed," he agreed, "though what you have achieved in such a short amount of time is nothing short of remarkable. Now show me again how I must move my feet."

"I would never have believed you would make such a handsome lad," Stephen said as they rode together down the track from Wensley village. "My only hope is that Lord Oliver is equally fooled."

"Of course he will be," Ella assured him. "People see what they expect to see. Lord Oliver is expecting to see you and your young ward, Eddie and that is what he will see."

"The addition of the bum fluff stuck to your chin was a masterstroke," he conceded. "Though I wonder if it will tickle my chin when I kiss you."

"You will never find out," she replied. "There will be no kissing while I am attired thus," she indicated her clothing." She wore the cream trousers and highly polished hessians worn by many young men, her linen shirt and waistcoat were covered by a tailcoat and topped by a thick overcoat to ward off the winter chill. Her hair had been fashioned into a long queue held in place by a simple black ribbon; the look was completed with the addition of a beaver hat.

"I admit that the fluff on your face should be enough to distract Lord Oliver from considering you as a woman."

"As well as taking his eyes, hopefully away from the scars, if he knows who I am, he surely knows about the scars," Ella replied.

"The scars are barely visible," he replied, "as are your delightful breasts," he leered outrageously. "What have you done with them?"

"They are tightly bound, duke. One could not risk having

them bouncing around," she replied, demurely. "Now, let us make haste, the sooner this starts, the sooner it finishes." She kicked her horse and galloped ahead.

Ella pulled up her horse as the stark ramparts of Bolton Castle reared before them. "It looks quite foreboding," she said quietly.

"I imagine it was meant to look so, nothing like putting the fear of God into your enemies before a shot is fired," Stephen replied. They looked at the building for a moment before Ella said, "Shall we?"

The first banquet was already in progress as they made their way into the great hall, a reminder of the castle's days as a Norman stronghold. A high table had been placed on a dais at the end of the room and trestle tables had been laid down the length of the hall. The luxurious Persian rugs and comfortable furniture had been removed to create what Lord Oliver clearly believed was a replica of a Tudor banquet. To the side of the high table was an ornate cradle by which sat a young woman, occasionally looking into it. "Ah," Stephen said quietly, "a redheaded babe, far easier to pass off as a descendent of the old queen and far less bother." At that point the child let out a high-pitched wail and the young woman plucked it from the cradle and proceeded to nurse it.

"See, our true king makes his presence heard."

Ella sucked in a breath as there was no doubting the owner of the voice. "Lord Oliver," she whispered.

"Ah, Hart," Lord Oliver spoke. "You are most welcome, Your Grace. Have no fear, you are among friends. We are men of a similar nature, ambitions and beliefs are we not?" He gestured to the men around him who responded by raising their goblets of wine. "Come," he continued, "we are honoured that one of your station has joined our number."

"Sit down here," Stephen said quietly as they passed a space at one of the lower tables, "learn what you can but try not to draw attention to yourself."

"Lord Richard Lonsdale," the young man opposite her said, offering his hand.

"Edward Gainsborough," she replied, shaking his hand with what she hoped was a firm enough grasp. "Mostly people call me Eddie."

The young man looked towards the high table where Stephen was now seated and drinking a cup of wine, "So what is your connection to the duke?"

"I am his ward," Ella replied. "My father served in his regiment, when he was killed, the duke promised that he would look after my mother and my sisters. I never knew my father."

"The duke must have known your father well," the young man replied. "Many soldiers die in the thick of battle but rarely do dukes bother to raise their families."

"My father was killed by a shot aimed at the duke," Ella improvised. "He was a brave man," she added.

"Brave indeed," the young man said, finally satisfied. "My father died racing a horse, stupid fellow. The jump was too high, my mother saw it, I saw it, even the horse saw it. The only one who was stupid enough not to see it was my father. The horse stopped but he did not. Landed on his head and that was that. Terrible mess." The young man took a drink of wine, and was, as Ella suspected, well into his cups.

Ella looked around, there were probably twenty or so men eating and drinking. "So is this the assembled company?" she asked.

"Apparently so," Lord Lonsdale replied. "Thought there would be more myself, and Oliver was definitely expecting more but that is what happens when you arrange a meeting in a

Godforsaken corner of Yorkshire in the middle of winter. Some cannot get here because of mud and others because of snow, though some more are expected tomorrow in time for the Masquerade where the final plans will be revealed."

Ella nodded and raised her cup of wine. "To success," she said.

"To success," he agreed, though he did not know of course that they were not toasting the same success.

CHAPTER 29

Ella hesitated at the foot of the spiral staircase leading up to the turret where she suspected that the Earl of Bolton, and owner of the castle, was imprisoned. She had left the great hall when those around her were either so drunk they were in danger of falling asleep at the table or had already left to retire to their chambers. Stephen, she noticed was deep in conversation with Lord Oliver and another man she had not seen before. She carefully carried the cup of wine up the stairs and had not gone beyond halfway when a voice thundered, "Who's there? Identify yourself."

"It's just me, Sir. Lord Oliver sent a cup of wine for you," she replied, running up the remaining steps.

"'E ain't never done that before."

"He thinks you've done a good job and that you should be rewarded," she replied, holding out the cup. It was the bear of a man Barbara had described when she had taken the tray of food up to whoever was in the tower.

"Well, I'm expectin' a bit more than a cup of wine, I don't even like wine, a cup of ale would 'ave been better," the man grumbled.

"Should I take it back then?" Ella asked, reaching for the cup.

"Nay, don't be so 'asty lad. No point in upsettin' 'is lordship is there?" He took a long draught.

"What are you doing up here anyway?" Ella asked. "Is this where the lord keeps his treasure?"

"No-one to bother yer young 'ead about, treasure indeed." He took another long swig. "'Ere." he held out the cup for Ella to take, before falling back onto the wooden chair.

Ella waited for a few seconds to ensure that the sleeping draught had taken full effect before gently taking the key from the man's leather belt and inserting it into the lock and pushing the stout door open. It took a moment for her eyes to adjust to the dim light, a single candle stood by the bed and she could just make out the shape of someone lying in the tangled sheets.

"Peter," she said quietly. There was no response. "Peter," she tried again.

The man on the bed sat up, "What the devil?"

"Peter, it is me, Ella Grainger," she explained, quickly going over to the bed. "Do you remember me?"

Peter nodded. "You played with me when we were young, you had a scar down the side of your face which my mother said I was not to mention." He peered at her closely. "It seems to have gone. But why are you here and why are you dressed as a man? Have you come to rescue me? Because if you have, you are going to need something with which to cut these." He held up his right hand, which Ella had not noticed was chained to the bedpost.

"It is a long story, and I am here to rescue you, but not tonight, I shall return tomorrow and you will be free. The Duke of Hart is leading a mission to avert Lord Oliver and his conspirators."

"Lord Oliver is a dangerous man." Peter's face turned white at his name. "I thought he was my friend, but all he wanted was the castle. I am surprised he has not had me killed already."

"He must have some purpose for you yet."

"I do not know what, for since he came here I have been a

prisoner. When he told me of his plans I was horrified and refused to have anything to do with them. I would never do anything against the crown."

Ella thought for a moment. "Mayhap Lord Oliver has something with which to bargain with you so that you do what he wishes. Your title is an old and powerful one and could be useful in drawing others to his cause."

Peter shook his head. "He knows."

"What does he know?"

The young man grasped her hand, his eyes were filled with fear, and shame. "He knows why I am unwed," he paused. "He knows that I am not attracted to women."

"How does he know?"

"I thought he was of like mind, he gave me the impression he was, but it was just a way to compromise me so that he could hold it over my head, to be revealed when he wants to. If he chooses to reveal my secret life my family is ruined and I shall be executed," he stated bleakly.

Ella nodded. "So in order to ensure your obedience, Lord Oliver has blackmailed you and kept you a prisoner but kept you alive so that you may be of use to him."

Peter nodded. "And I suspect, has used the money from my estates to finance his deeds, the bastard."

"Quite," Ella replied, crisply. "However, his scheming will come to nothing. There are men loyal to the monarch who will be launching an attack tomorrow night, the night of the Masquerade, we shall rescue you and Lord Oliver, and his friends will be brought to justice."

"Can you not release me now?"

She shook her head. "We cannot risk Lord Oliver suspecting anything. I just wanted you to know that you will soon be safe, but you must ensure you do not say anything to arouse suspicion."

"Thank you." He hesitated, then added, "And you will not say aught of my...tastes?"

Ella shrugged "We had two footmen who had similar tastes, father did not notice and the rest of us did not care. They were kind and gentle men, and everyone liked them. I imagine it is something you cannot help for if you could choose, I doubt you would, given the difficult life it forces upon you."

"Thank you once again."

Ella looked towards the door. "I must go now. The sleeping draught I gave to your guard will not last long." She leaned forward and hugged her childhood friend. "Until tomorrow." He nodded.

"Ella," he said, as she reached the door. "I am sorry I shoved you in the priest hole when we were children."

She grinned. "You have no idea how useful that experience proved to be."

The guard was still snoring as she locked the door and replaced the key on his belt before retrieving the empty cup and quietly making her way down the stairs. The great hall was empty save for a couple of servants sweeping the floor as she passed through on her way to her room, she was glad to see that Barbara was not among them.

"Where have you been?" Stephen hissed as she entered her room. He was sitting in the chair, his feet propped against the fireplace, apparently relaxed, but she knew better.

"I was right. Peter, the Earl of Bolton is here, under lock and key."

"And how did you find this information?" he asked.

"I went to the tower and spoke with him."

"You did what?" Stephen's voice was barely above a whisper though it felt like a shout.

"I gave his guard a cup of drugged wine, took the key and found Peter in the tower. He is chained to the bedpost so we shall have to ensure that we can cut him free, although I may be able to pick the lock with a hairpin." Her words ground to a halt when she saw his stern expression. "What?"

Stephen shook his head. "You would not last five minutes as a soldier because you do not seem to understand the concept of obeying orders."

"I did not disobey any orders," she countered. "No-one said I should not go to the tower and search for the earl."

"Only because no-one thought it would occur to you to do so."

"Well, the point is, Peter is being held against his will, apparently when Lord Oliver realised he would have no part in the uprising, he was locked in the tower, but he obviously thinks there is still some value in him because he's still alive. Oliver is blackmailing him. I told him we would rescue him tomorrow."

Stephen quirked an eyebrow. "So now you are giving orders? Blackmail you say?"

She took a breath. "Lord Oliver has found out that Peter, shall we say, prefers the company of men to women and has threatened to expose him if he does not do as he says. The scandal would ruin Peter's family to say nothing of the fact that he would be executed. I can only surmise that Lord Oliver believes he can coerce Peter into pretending at least to support the cause thus encouraging other powerful men who are currently sitting on the fence to see whether the revolution has a chance of success. Or it will at the very least enhance their grip on wealth and power."

Stephen nodded. "You are right, the earl needs to be rescued even before we spring our attack. His knowledge of the castle could prove useful."

"Perhaps I could be trusted with the matter, if we rescue him just as the guests are going down to the tunnels for the revelry, everyone will be occupied so no-one will check on the earl. It was an easy enough matter to get to him tonight," she suggested.

Stephen looked into her eyes. "Do not make the mistake of assuming that you will get away tomorrow with what you got away with tonight. The earl's guard may not take a cup from you, what then?"

"I shall use my initiative," she replied, evenly. "In any case, you do not have spare men to assign to the task."

"Very well, but if there is a hint of things going awry, you are to get out of there immediately, do you understand?" He drew her into his arms. "I could not bear it if a single hair on your head is injured."

She nodded. "What did you find out from Lord Oliver?" she asked, changing the subject before Stephen changed his mind.

He ran a hand through his hair. "Nothing of great significance, he gave little away, but he is no lord, that I do know. He claims to have an estate in Hampshire, but I have never heard of it or of the Oliver family and I have connections with many of the families from that county. He claims to have served in the army but had little knowledge of the regiment he claimed to serve in, the 37th North Hampshire Hussars.

"And you do know about it?"

"It was the family regiment, if Cameron did join the army, that would have been the one he would have served with."

"But you said there was no record of him," she said.

"There are many ways a man may serve the army, some overt and some covert, it may have been that my brother was engaged in some activity behind enemy lines. Had the enemy captured him and found out he was the son of a duke, he would have been a very valuable prisoner."

"I see."

"There is something about the man that does not ring true, but he is a cold, cruel and calculating bastard, of that I am sure. He is a man of great ambition and will do anything to achieve it, this much we already know. Until he is safely brought to justice no-one is safe, not you, not I, not the king and especially not that innocent babe he is using as a pawn in his game. Now, here is the final plan and this is what I want you to do..."

CHAPTER 30

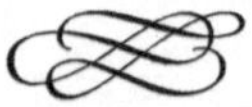

Ella waited until she heard the men leaving the great hall and heading towards the entrance to the tunnels, judging by the noise, they had already imbibed a great deal of the earl's finest wines. They were all masked, as was she. Her mask was a simple black silk, tied at the back. She had eschewed the cloak as it might restrict her movements should she need to move quickly. She picked up the cup of wine and headed towards the spiral staircase which led to the tower. She had only taken three steps when the familiar voice boomed. "Who goes there? Identify yourself."

"It is I sir, young Eddie. I brought you the drink from Lord Oliver last night and he sent me with more for you tonight," she replied.

"Come then."

She had barely reached the top step when the cup was dashed from her hand and the brute had his hand around her throat, forcing her back to the wall. "That weren't sent by 'is lordship and neither is this, think yer can get away with druggin' me a second time?" he snarled. "So who are yer? If yer thinkin' of rescuing the young earl, think again, ain't nobody gets past me," his rancid breath assaulted her nostrils.

Only one of his meaty hands was around her throat, the other held her other hand above her head, pinning her to the cold, stone wall so the move that had been so successful against Lord Willoughby was not an option. "I got past you once," she whispered with what little breath she had, "and I shall do it again. Old fashioned though this be..." She aimed a carefully positioned kick at his groin which caused him to let out a bellow and release her. It did not take long for him to recover and charge towards her, a thick cudgel raised over his head.

She positioned herself at the top of the staircase and at the last second leapt out of the way, stuck her foot out and he tumbled headfirst down the stone staircase, his large body thudding against every step until, with a sickening crack, he reached the bottom.

Ella waited for several seconds, then, hearing nothing, tentatively walked down the stairs. His eyes were closed, but she was relieved to see the steady rise and fall of his chest. It would no doubt have been a quicker and less painful death than he would have given her, but it was the first time that she had used her skills in anything other than an exhibition and she had to take deep breaths to get her heart under control. Killing a man was not something she ever wished to do, though it was something she knew she might have to do tonight. Hopefully she would have enough time to release Peter and make their escape before he regained consciousness, she reached for his belt and took the key to the tower.

Peter sat up as she entered. "Ella, is that you? What the devil is going on? What did you do to Brutus?"

"Brutus? Aptly named," she replied, hurrying over to the bed and removing a pin from her hair.

"It is what I call him at any rate. I heard a great commotion."

"Well, suffice it to say, Brutus will not be bothering anyone for now at any rate," she explained, inserting the pin into the lock and twisting it.

Peter's eyes widened. "You killed him?"

"He lost his balance and fell down the stairs, I imagine he will awaken with the mother of all headaches which will no doubt make him even more unpleasant than he already is," she explained, deciding to leave the matter at that. The lock clicked and sprung open. "Come, there is limited time and I need you to do something."

"Anything," he replied, rubbing some feeling back into his wrist.

"The conspirators are to be captured tonight. I need you to go to the tunnel which has an entrance in the escarpment and open the gate, there will be men waiting there to gain entry. Then, lead them down the tunnel to the great chamber where the Duke of Hart and his men will be waiting."

"That entrance has not been used for years, I do not even know if the tunnel still stands, or indeed if the entrance is not overgrown," he replied.

"We must hope that it does, I have recently been in many of the other tunnels and all of them were navigable," she admitted.

He frowned. "How?"

She gave him a sly grin. "I worked here as a maid for a short while, which is how I discovered that you were being kept prisoner in your own castle."

His eyebrows shot up. "A maid?"

"A maid," she confirmed. "Truth to tell, I was a very good maid, and it certainly gave me renewed respect for those who work so hard so that we do not have to. I shall tell you the whole tale one day, but we do not have much time. We must make haste. I shall go down to the tunnel which leads to the church and open the door so that the other group of men may enter and we may rid ourselves of this heinous plot and the wicked Lord Oliver."

"Amen to that."

The route to the church tunnel took Ella through the main chamber. She was surprised to see that there were about forty men gathered, more than she had been expecting. The tables were laden with huge joints of meat, beef, lamb and what looked suspiciously like a swan, there were large jugs of sauce and in front of each man was a trencher, no doubt meant to remind the men of the link to the Tudor dynasty. Young women, she assumed from the surrounding village, walked around the chamber pouring wine into pewter cups. She kept to the edges of the chamber hoping that no-one would notice her, their attention mostly being on the young women and which man could pull their bodices down to expose their breasts to the amusement of all.

"Ah, it is the young ward of the duke here is it not?" She froze at the sound of Lord Oliver's voice. "Come, join us."

She walked towards him and bowed. "Thank you, my lord, it will be an honour," she replied, trying to keep the tremor from her voice.

He turned to Stephen. "I am curious to know why this young man did not join us earlier. Did you not think he could be trusted?"

"I would not have brought him, Oliver, if I did not think he could be trusted," Stephen replied evenly.

"Tell me, young man. Why were you scurrying through the tunnel as though your life depends upon it?"

"I was curious, my lord. I had heard of the tunnels and wanted to see them for myself. I did not mean to offend," Ella replied. "I apologise for interrupting your revels, I should take my leave."

The hand that landed on her shoulder gripped hard. "Nonsense, young man, you may stay and enjoy the spectacle," Lord Oliver replied, a gleam in his eye. "I can guarantee you will find the entertainment diverting." He turned to Stephen, "Really, Your

Grace, did you think our revels here tonight would debauch your young ward? Surely he is near enough of age to enjoy the pleasures of good wine, the company of beautiful women and the discussion of men of vision."

"Indeed, Lord Oliver, though this is Eddie's first foray into society, I thought perhaps the meat a little too rich for him on this occasion." He turned to Ella. "Perhaps it is time for you to return to your chamber, I believe you are not too young to join the hunt tomorrow."

"As your host, I must insist that your young ward joins us," Lord Oliver said smoothly, waving a hand to summon one of the women. "Pour this young man a cup of wine," he commanded. "I do not wish him to miss the excitement of the evening."

Ella glanced at Stephen, something was amiss, something about Lord Oliver's demeanour raised the alarm bells as surely as if they were standing in a church tower. He clearly knew something, though they did not know what or how much, but it seemed that he knew something of their plans. "Thank you, my lord," Ella replied, taking the cup, "it is generous of you to allow me to join the party."

"I can confidently say that you will remember this night for the rest of your life," he replied, touching her cup with his." Drink," he commanded.

Ella raised the cup to her lips, took a swig and replaced it on the table, before reaching for a slice of beef with her knife and tipping the cup over. "I am sorry, my lord, I am not usually such a clodpole." She did not attempt to mop up the mess, thinking that was something a young woman might do, but not a young man. Lord Oliver shrugged. "It is of little consequence. Ah," his eyes lit up. "The first part of the entertainment is about to start. You should enjoy this young Eddie."

Ella looked up as several scantily clad young women entered the chamber. The musicians began to strike up a tune, and the women began to dance, seductively twining themselves around as many men as they could as they weaved their way around the chamber. She was amazed to see them removing articles of clothing or encouraging the men to do so as they danced. At the end of the dance the women were almost completely naked, standing in a tableau to the roar of approval from the men. Lord Oliver banged on the table. "Gentlemen, gentlemen, these ladies will remain here for your entertainment. They have been paid well to cater to your every whim. Those of you who have not yet signed the document of loyalty to the rightful king, the babe you saw yesterday need to do so now. Tomorrow, we ride to Manchester to meet with our brothers who are, as we speak, enlisting the support of factory and foundry workers to our cause." There was a resounding shout from the men. He turned to Stephen. "Shall we?" He gestured for Stephen to precede him. He pointed to Ella. "And you, young sir."

Lord Oliver gestured to the two men who had stood sentinel behind his chair, and they fell in line behind the three of them. Ella and Stephen exchanged a glance as things were not going according to plan. As they walked down the tunnel towards the castle, noise could still be heard from the chamber, but it was not the sound of steel on steel, where were Stephen's men? Ella had not been able to reach the church entrance, but Peter should have reached the escarpment by now and led those men through to the chamber. They walked on in silence until they reached the library where a fire and many candles had been lit.

"Brandy?" Lord Oliver asked.

"No thank you," Stephen replied smoothly. "Let us get on and sign the document, then we may return to the carousing."

Lord Oliver sat behind the desk and steepled his fingers, his eyes narrowed. "Somehow I do not feel that you are entirely loyal to the cause, Hart."

"Then why did you invite me to be a part of it?" Stephen shot back. "You did not invite me by chance, I imagine that you felt I would be a useful ally to have, a powerful voice on your side."

"Indeed, but all the brothers have had to prove their allegiance, an initiation if you will and so, it seems must you."

"And how would you like me to do that?"

"Simple," the other man smiled, reaching into the drawer and retrieving a pistol. "I want you to kill your young ward."

CHAPTER 31

"What?" The single syllable bounced around the room.

"If you wish to be accepted into the brotherhood, you must kill your ward. He is an orphan is he not? No-one shall miss him. He means nothing to anyone. In all honesty some of the other brothers have had to do worse, I am giving you an easy assignment." Lord Oliver sounded almost bored, yet his knuckles were white as he gripped the pistol. His eyes narrowed. "Or is there more to your relationship with the boy? My, my what a scandal that would make."

"Are you mad?" Stephen said, moving to stand in front of Ella. "How does killing a young boy prove loyalty?"

"To become a brother, one must be willing to sacrifice everything for the cause. I am disappointed but not surprised Hart, for now I shall have to kill both of you," Lord Oliver drawled, levelling the pistol at Stephen's chest. "It will be a pleasure."

"No," Ella screamed as Stephen hit the ground, there was no time to do anything else. When she saw him start to dive, she moved. The sound was barely out of her mouth before she sprinted forward, leapt over the desk and landed on Lord Oliver with her feet planted firmly on his chest. They both fell to the ground as the chair toppled over. There was a crack as the pistol discharged and plaster fell from the ceiling.

"You murderous snake," Ella hissed. "Your days are numbered, my lord." She twisted his arm and stood behind him, giving him the same warning she had given Stephen when she had demonstrated her combat skills to him a few weeks ago. "If you struggle my lord, your arm will come out of its socket and will hang uselessly by your side, it will also be excruciatingly painful, though it can be repaired and for the most part, people get most of the use back in their arm."

"I suggest you look to the front young man, or should I say Lady Ella," Lord Oliver drawled.

Ella could not suppress a slight gasp at the sight of Stephen held by the two burly henchmen, one of whom held a knife to his throat.

"I suggest you release me within the next moment, or your precious duke here will bleed his life out right now," he continued.

"Don't let him go..." Stephen managed to speak, before one of the men hit him with a cudgel and he fell to the ground.

"Now Lady Ella, I doubt, even given your skills you will be able to conquer all of us," Lord Oliver's tone was amused, "so I suggest you release me. It will of course have no influence on the outcome as neither of you will be leaving this room alive, although," his eyes narrowed, "the sight of a powerful duke bound and held prisoner might inspire some of the peasants to our side. It is not quite the treatment the French aristocracy endured but it is a start. In fact," he warmed to his theme, "it would make a considerable impact should your duke here be dragged through the streets to his execution, the first execution of the new regime, that should inspire the poor and be a timely reminder to the nobility on which side to place their allegiance, and he wouldn't be the first duke I have killed. Violence and fear are, after all, the tools of any revolution. You however," he turned his head towards her, "have no use whatsoever. Now, if you would be so good as to release me before I change my mind and have your duke finished off."

Ella gave his arm a twist before releasing it, causing him to roar in pain as it fell weakly to his side. "You bitch," he shouted. "I had thought to make it easy for you by making your death quick but now I think not, now I think I shall give you to the men to play with before killing you myself, slowly and painfully."

"Do what you will," she shot back, "at least you will not be able to use that arm to injure others."

He took a step forward and picked up his knife from the desk. "I have a good mind to finish you now." He held the knife to her throat with his other hand, and Ella could feel the prick of its tip as he drew a drop of blood. "I have often wondered whether it is in fact possible to inflict death by a thousand cuts," he mused. He drew the knife back for a second cut when the door was flung open.

"My lord, my lord, you must come, there is hell down in the chamber." The young man staggered into the room, blood streaming from a deep cut on his forehead, his breath coming in short gasps. "They came from nowhere, one minute we were drinking and playing with the women and the next they were on us. It is carnage, my lord."

"What the devil?" Lord Oliver bellowed, turning to Ella. "This is your doing, I do not know how, but I know you being here is no coincidence."

"What can you mean Lord Oliver?" she replied. "What could I possibly have to do with armed men attacking your renegades? I am, after all, a weak and fragile woman."

"You. You were the reason I had to leave the service of the duke," he shouted, pointing to Stephen. "This one's brother. Had it not been for your meddling and interfering I should have taken enough money to live my life in luxury. His Grace had no idea until you looked at the ledgers, I could have gone on for years. It was you, poking your nose into his accounts that ruined me, leaving me without employment, a character, I almost ended up in the poor house.

"You rich people think that being born in the right bed gives you the right to rule and the rest of us should be content with the crumbs from your table. But I have cunning and I have nerve. I did not wait for opportunity to come to me. I went out and took it as His Grace's brother found out. The Thorne brothers have been exactly that a thorn in my side, well the oldest brother is in a shallow grave in the Pyrenees where no-one shall find him, he caught me taking what was rightfully mine, legitimate treasure from the church so I did for him. And I shall have my revenge on you, make no mistake, my lady. Your father was right. You should have perished in the fire that so disfigured you that no man would look at you. Perhaps if you had attracted the interest of a man, you would not have poked your nose into business that did not concern you."

"My lord," the young man said, "please, your men need you to lead them."

"Tie her up," he ordered the men standing by Stephen, "then join me."

"What about this one?" one of the men asked, nudging Stephen with his boot.

"Leave him, he will not be going anywhere soon. I shall deal with them both when we have quelled whatever is happening in the tunnels. Join me when you have done." He swept from the room holding his arm Ella noted with a degree of satisfaction.

The men did not take long in their eagerness to get to the fighting, nor did they notice the way Ella held her hands while they were tying them, although it looked as though her palms were together, she managed to create a small space which meant that with a little wriggling, when they had gone, eager to join the fray, she was able to loosen her bonds.

"Stephen, Stephen, please, you need to wake up." She shook his shoulder. "Please Stephen, my love we need you...I need you. After all we have been through I cannot bear the thought of you not by my side. I love you Stephen Thorne and I am not going to lose you again."

She was rewarded with a groan and his eyes opened. "Oh, thank God." She took his face in her hands and kissed him.

"Well," he replied with a lopsided grin, "I should be unconscious more often if this is the reward I get when I come round." He tentatively touched the back of his head. "I am assuming that one of the two charming gentlemen holding a knife to my throat hit me with what feels like a battering ram."

She nodded. "Are you able to stand?"

He nodded then grimaced. "It hurts like the devil, but I expect I shall survive." He levered himself upright. "Where is that viper Oliver?"

"I believe your men have broken through, a messenger came and said there was trouble. I am sorry, I let you down, I could not get to the church to let the reinforcements in."

He took her by the shoulders. "Ella, do not think that, for God's sake you leapt in front of me to take a bullet that was meant for me, which by the way, you are never to do anything like it again. I could not live with myself if something happened to you, nor," he added, "should I want to." He kissed her forehead. "Now, I think we must get down to the tunnels and see what awaits us there."

Ella laid a hand on his arm. "Oliver is no lord, apparently, he was the man who was stealing from Elliott, the man I discovered, that is how he knew who I was and why he wants revenge. He said I had ruined his life and that he will have his revenge. His name is

Jonathon Reece, and he was to oversee Elliot's purchases for his various commercial enterprises. I found him out because he was sending larger bills to clients than he was recording as well as claiming items cost more than he was recording in the ledgers and pocketing the quite sizeable difference. I found copies of the invoices he both, received and sent and checked them against the ledgers. I was suspicious and wrote to the businesses involved which confirmed my suspicions. I took the evidence to Elliot and he dismissed him."

"That goes some way to explain at least his animosity towards you," Stephen mused, checking his pistol and tucking his knife back into his boot.

"I imagine he also holds a generous grudge against powerful people such as Elliott and yourself who can ruin people's lives on a whim if they so choose, though in his case his dismissal was entirely of his own making, and would have been worse had Elliott chosen to report his crime to the magistrate." She paused. "There is more. Apparently, your brother, Cameron came across him in the army and caught him stealing from a church, I am sorry, but he killed him, Stephen. Cameron is buried in a shallow grave in the Pyrenees."

Stephen nodded. "Then let us ensure that the bastard pays for his crimes."

As they approached the entrance to the tunnel Stephen paused. "Please stay behind me when we enter, Ella."

She nodded. "All right, being as you asked rather than commanded." She could not resist a small grin.

He shook his head, grimaced at the pain that shot through his temple and threw open the oak door. The scene of revelry had been changed for one of carnage, tables and chairs had been overthrown and wine flowed onto the floor where barrels had been toppled, mingling with the blood of the dead and injured. Several men were on the floor, some were groaning and others deathly silent, others were seated with their backs against the wall with their hands tied behind their backs, several gashes, cuts and bruises on their faces. Stephen's men were taking the names of the conspirators. Peter, his face flushed with a mixture of exertion and excitement rushed up to them.

"Congratulations, Your Grace, the revolution has been stopped and the conspirators routed," he said, holding out his hand.

"Let us hope so." Stephen took his hand and shook it. "Did any escape?"

Peter nodded. "A small cohort escaped back down the tunnel towards the escarpment."

"I imagine they took the horses that were tethered there and are on their way over the Pennines, possibly to Manchester or Liverpool where they will be able to lay low. Where is the man who calls himself Lord Oliver?"

Peter looked at his feet. "I regret to say that he was one of the few who escaped, though not without sustaining an injury to his arm, I doubt he will be able to ride for long."

"We shall find him, and we have Ella to thank for his inability to sit a horse for long," Stephen replied.

Peter looked at Ella with a grin. "Well, I cannot say I am surprised, given that she dealt with Brutus without batting an eyelid. She is a singular kind of woman."

"That she is," Stephen agreed wholeheartedly.

CHAPTER 32

"I cannot believe we lost him," Ella said, drawing back her bow and letting the arrow fly.

"I imagine he had a safe house or series of safe houses to go to," Stephen replied. "Not bad," he added, looking at the target.

"Where do you think he will go?" She pulled another arrow from the quiver and placed it on the nock.

"If he intends to escape abroad, we have men at Dover and Portsmouth and Tilbury if the continent is his aim, as well as Southampton and Liverpool should he attempt to cross to the New World."

"He is quite deranged," Ella replied, taking aim and letting another arrow fly. "I doubt that he will give up on his plan so easily."

Stephen shook his head. "His circle of conspirators is broken, he has neither the men nor the funds to carry out his dastardly plan, but rest assured, we will find him and bring him to justice."

"What do you think he meant when he said 'as His Grace's brother found out? Do you think he knows something about Cameron?"

Stephen shook his head. "I do not know, but I fully intend to find out."

She turned to him. "Thank God young Harry has been returned to his parents, I doubt Reece would have let him live long after his usefulness had worn out," she said then paused. "I have another question."

"Go on."

"Why are we here, at Wensley? Why are we not giving chase to Jonathon Reece now we know his real name?"

Stephen looked around at the lush green countryside that surrounded his estate. "I think we deserve the opportunity to both rest and regroup after the mission, as well as take stock of what we discovered. There are agents all over the country on the lookout for Reece, but bear in mind he may have already taken on a new identity now that his alias of Lord Oliver is known. I receive reports regularly, any sighting and we shall be able to capture him, hopefully without the need for bloodshed."

"Had it not been for Peter's quick thinking in letting in your men from the church when he realised I had not been able to, there would have been more bloodshed," she said quietly.

"Indeed. We lost several good men that day," he replied solemnly. "However," he added, "men who sign up to do the work I do know the risks and are prepared to take them for the sake of the country."

"I know," she replied, turning away so he could not see the tears in her eyes. "I understand that it is just that..."

"That what?" he asked.

"I cannot bear to think of the danger you willingly put yourself in," she replied. "I cannot bear to think of you being injured or killed Stephen. I know we have not always seen eye to eye, but, contrary to all my expectations, I like you. There, I said it."

"You like me?"

"I said so, did I not?"

"Well, they are words I never expected to hear," he chuckled.

"I would also point out that you did no less in terms of putting your own life in danger. As it happens Lady Ella, I like you too, rather too much I think and when all this is over and Reece is finally given his just desserts, I very much want you to become my duchess Ella. I like to think of myself as an honourable man, and I want to do the right thing."

She raised an eyebrow. "The right thing?"

"I have bedded you," he said, simply. "It was not my intention to dishonour you but in the excitement of the mission I did not exercise self-discipline, therefore, we must marry."

"Do not dare to apologise for what we did," she shot back, angrily. "I am a grown woman, and it was my decision to make love with you. Do not make it sound small and sordid."

He stepped back to look at her. "Ella, you are wonderful and I lo...."

She placed her hand on his lips, "Do not say anything you might later come to regret, people say all manner of things when life is not normal. We have not lived in normal times since this adventure began. And I will not marry a man, duke or servant who believes he must marry me because of his honour. He will love me with passion, or I shall not marry at all."

"Very well." He sighed and added, "but when we return to normality, there is a conversation that must be had."

"I have yet another question," she said, deciding to change what was becoming an uncomfortable subject.

"And that is?"

"Why are we doing this?" She gestured with the longbow. "I doubt we shall be called upon to use this weapon. In fact, I believe it reached its zenith in 1415 at the battle of Agincourt, and I do not believe archers have been used in battle since the 1500's."

He grinned wolfishly. "It is so I can do this." He stepped closer as his arms went around her and drew her towards his body so that she could feel his arousal through the thickness of her skirts and the thought of his arousal quickly awakened her own. He placed one hand over hers as they drew back the bow between them, the arrow arced through the air and landed with a thud in the centre of the target. "Bullseye," he said, taking her hand, "now, come with me."

They raced back towards the house, but instead of entering by the large oak door, they went down the side and entered the orangerie. The scent of citrus hit her as they closed the door behind them. The glass walls were almost covered by the large fronds of greenery and in the centre a small fountain played. All around were trees bearing oranges and lemons with small exotic flowers growing at their roots. Stephen led her to a wrought iron bench and they sat down. She fully expected him to kiss her and could not help but feel disappointed when he merely turned to her. "I have something to show you," he said, drawing a letter from his pocket. "Here." He handed it to her.

Dear Hart,

We are pleased and delighted that as a result of your loyal service, a catastrophe for us and the country has been averted. Due to your diligence, duty and determination, the crisis has passed without most of our subjects knowing. We need not tell you of the dark days that would have enveloped the country should it have been plunged into civil war. We understand that most of the would-be traitors have been apprehended and will face the full force of British justice due to the bravery of your men. However, we are also given to understand that a crucial person in your endeavours was Lady Eleanor Grainger, daughter of the late Earl. We find ourselves fascinated that a woman could add so much to your mission that we summon you and Lady Grainger to attend us at Carlton House to relate to us in person the details of the mission. We also look forward to hearing that the ringleader has also been apprehended. We shall expect you to attend us at the end of the month.

George R

"It is from the king," Ella said, catching her breath.

"Evidently," he agreed.

"But how does he know of my involvement? You told him?" Her eyes were wide.

"I did," he said. "I remember a conversation not long ago when you were quite specific about the fact that women's lives were made small by the restrictions placed on them by society. You were quite right and I thought the king should know that in denying women at least some of the freedoms and rights of men, he is depriving his kingdom of the talents and service of half of the population."

Much as it annoyed her, Ella could feel the prick of tears in her eyes. "Thank you," she whispered, "for having faith in me."

"Faith has nothing to do with it," he countered. "I saw with my own eyes your talent for deciphering a code and felt with my own bones your talent in martial art. I have just witnessed your quick mastery of archery and although I have not witnessed it directly, I am certain your swordsmanship is equally impressive. I judged you on evidence, nothing less."

"And do you think this will change society with regard to how women are perceived and what they are allowed to achieve?"

He shook his head. "In all honesty, I doubt it. We men have had the upper hand for too long for us to relinquish it lightly. However, a pebble thrown into a pool ripples out until the ripples reach the shore, so let us just say, a pebble has been thrown into a pool and one day, the ripples may change society's attitudes for those of your gender."

Ella nodded. "You are correct, Rome, as they say, was not built in a day and even if the king is minded to make some changes, no doubt it may take time." She hissed in a breath. "But if we are to travel to London before the end of the month, we must make haste and what of Reece? Clearly the king expects us to have apprehended him before our audience."

"Indeed, we shall leave for the city as soon as the arrangements can be made, I shall send a message to open up the town house, and we shall depart as soon as we can. As for Reece, it would not surprise me if he had made his way to London where he can melt into the crowd until he wishes to strike."

"To strike?"

"His grand plan was to eliminate the king, and I suspect his heirs and successors, and, as we know, create himself king, rather like the emperors of ancient Rome. We managed to scupper his plan for revolution, but I imagine he has not given up on the assassination of the king, that in itself would create instability within the country and could lead to the uprising he still hopes to orchestrate. This is, of course, speculation on my part."

Ella nodded. "But, given Reece's fanatical zeal, quite reasonable speculation, and should his plan fail, he would no doubt attempt to slip out of the country on a ship from Tilbury or any port and escape justice."

Stephen grimaced. "We cannot rest until he is either apprehended or dead."

Ella stood and held out her hand. "Come," she said.

He quirked an eyebrow in question.

"All this talk of death has made me want to feel alive. I want to feel your hands and mouth on my body, skin to skin. In short, I want you to make love to me Stephen."

"Oh God," he said quietly, "I shall never be able to resist you."

CHAPTER 33

Ella had kept her eyes closed for much of the journey from Wensleydale, not because she was sleeping but because she wanted to commit to memory every second of the three days they had spent together preparing for their departure to London. It had been the most delicious of dreams, a private world in which she and Stephen had spent their waking and sleeping moments together. They had ridden together, walked, dined and talked of anything and everything from politics to the correct way to eat a scone with jam and cream. They had read together in the library and worked together, he at his government papers and she preparing a book of puzzles for children he had encouraged her to write, Stephen had suggested the title of 'Ella's Enigmas'.

The nights had passed in a blur of kisses and caresses as he had kissed everywhere on her body and explored every inch of her skin and she his, as they both reached peak after peak of pleasure until they fell asleep satiated and exhausted but still desperate for each other. She had loved it all, the quiet times, the laughter, the excitement of working together, the discussions and the passion, her world had gone from the quiet life of a spinster, companion to her aunt to the thrill of a working on a mission on behalf of the king and the love she felt for Stephen. Her thoughts screeched to a halt. Was what she felt for Stephen love? She had never thought she would love someone and certainly it had been drilled into her that no man would ever love her, ugly and disfigured as she was. Indeed, no man before Stephen had ever shown the slightest interest in her, a cursory glance had been all she had been afforded before their eyes alighted on someone younger and prettier. She had long become accustomed to transforming from a wallflower to a full-blown spinster, but Stephen had seen through to the real her and she could not help but love him for it. On the other hand, they had just been through an exhilarating and, at times, terrifying experience and logic told her that both their emotions had been heightened. What she was feeling was probably not love, just reaction to a singular set of circumstances.

Stephen watched the emotions play across Ella's expressive face. She looked as though she was sleeping, but he knew she was not. The last three days had been perhaps the best days of his life, spent with the woman he loved, the woman he had always loved and the only woman he would ever love. For many years he had tried to forget her after she had refused his offer, but he could not, and yet the woman he thought he knew all those years ago was only a part of the woman she was today. Ella had opened his mind not only to the restrictions they were placed under, but what women could achieve, given the opportunities. It would be an uphill struggle to persuade the old fossils in parliament that a change in law was needed and an even steeper climb to tackle society's rules, but by God he would try and the first thing he would do is to persuade his contacts at the Diplomatic Office that women could and should play a vital part in their work.

He longed to stretch out and run his fingertip along her cheek to feel the silk of her skin, but did not want to interrupt her reverie. He fervently hoped that the time they had spent together showed her the life they could have as man and wife, he gloried in her wantonness in the bedroom, there would be no trouble in the getting of heirs, indeed there would be much enjoyment, but he had also loved their quieter moments, the way she absently twirled a stray lock of hair as she read or the way she stroked the quill across her chin as she considered what to write. He adored her fearlessness when they were riding, though his heart was in his mouth as she urged Beauty to jump a high hedge, he made a mental note to ensure all the fences, walls and hedges on his estates be kept to a reasonable height. All he had to do was to persuade her to become his wife, she had feelings for him, he knew in his heart, but he had to overcome the high tower of protection she had built around herself from childhood and he would do it if it was one brick at a time.

Stephen was suddenly aware that Ella's eyes were open. "Where are we?" she asked.

He looked out of the window. "I should say about an hour from Stamford where we shall stay for the night at The George. I sent a message two days ago to reserve accommodation and food. In fact," he consulted his pocket watch, "we may have time to stretch our legs and look about the town as we have made good time."

"I should like that," she replied, stretching her arms above her head and giving him the most delightful sight of her figure. "Much as I enjoy the excitement of seeing new places, I find the means of getting there less delightful."

"We could perhaps have travelled by canal, though I doubt it would have been much quicker, however, things are changing fast and one day, I believe we shall be able to travel by steam train at, they say, speeds of thirty miles an hour."

"My goodness, that would mean we should be able to travel from Yorkshire to London in a matter of hours."

"Indeed. Though in the here and now, we have arrived."

"It is an impressive and welcome sight," Ella said as she stepped down from the coach and looked at the stone building with fifteen windows overlooking the street.

"I believe an inn has stood on this spot for over a thousand years," he replied. "Hospitality was once offered by the Abbey which is long gone, and I am told that some of the structure dates back to the religious houses."

"Ah, Your Grace, welcome, welcome." A tall and well-rounded gentleman had opened the door and was advancing towards them.

Stephen shook his hand. "Thank you, John, the welcome at The George is always warm."

"It's always a pleasure to serve Your Grace, your rooms are prepared and a meal will be served as soon as you are ready in the private dining room. There is hot water should you wish to refresh yourselves from the journey."

"Half an hour should be plenty of time and I am looking forward to some of your excellent beef."

They walked through the public bar where several men were sitting at tables drinking pints of foaming ale and some eating generous plates of delicious smelling stew. Another man sat on his own with his back against the window, the light throwing him into silhouette. Ella turned, feeling she was being watched, and a shiver ran down her back. The lone man raised his tankard, obscuring his face, and took a long drink.

After washing and shaking the dust from her gown, Ella made her way to the private dining room. Stephen had secured the finest rooms at the inn, their two rooms separated by a sitting room with the dining room down the corridor. Stephen was already in the oak panelled dining room when she arrived. The table was set for two and almost groaning under the weight of the dishes. "I trust you are hungry as John and his wife have prepared a feast for us." He smiled, handing her a small glass of sherry.

"Quite famished," she replied, taking a sip.

When they were seated, Stephen lifted one of the cloches to reveal a tureen of white soup, there was also a fine stew of beef, carrots, onions and potatoes, another dish contained creamed cabbage. "My goodness," Ella murmured, "I rather think there is enough food here to feed an army, and a hungry one at that."

They ate in companionable silence before Stephen said, "As we have dined early, would you like to take a short stroll?"

Ella gently patted her stomach. "I think I shall need to. If I ate another bite, I am quite sure I should burst."

"It is a charming town," Ella remarked as they walked arm in arm along the cobbled High Street towards St. Michael the Greater Church. "Some of the buildings look as though they were built in Tudor times and yet there are other fine houses that are newly built."

"Apart from the time when the monasteries were closed, Stamford has always had a thriving economy based on cloth and glazed pottery. It is said that the barons met here before heading to Runnymede for the signing of the Magna Carta. During the Civil War it was held by the Parliamentarians, in fact Oliver Cromwell himself was the local commander." He looked sharply at Ella as she gave a small cry. "What? What is the matter, Ella?"

Her face was white,. "That man, the one sitting on his own when we entered the inn, it is him."

"What man?"

She took a deep breath, "There was a man sitting on his own by the window as we walked through the inn, his face was in shadow so it was difficult to see him well, I felt he was looking at us and he raised his tankard so that his face was further obscured, but I had a feeling I had seen him before. It was Reece, it was the name Oliver that prompted my memory." She turned. "Quickly, we must hurry back."

"Wait." He pulled her back. "We cannot just storm into the inn, for one thing we do not know if he is alone."

"Then what shall we do?"

He paused for a moment. "You will stand by the milliners we passed close to the inn, intent on looking at the bonnets but keeping an eye on the door. He will have to come out of it if he is to board the mail coach or some such, if he does you will have to detain him. I shall go into the bar and see if he is still there and if not enquire from John what time he left. If he is still in his room, I shall surprise him there and if not, I will catch him at the stable."

"I rather think the element of surprise is lost," she replied, "but thank you."

"For what?"

"For believing that I am capable on my own of detaining him if need be."

"We must do what we can, count to one hundred and if I have not returned, come into the inn." With that he ran across the cobbles towards The George.

To all intents and purposes Ella was a woman absorbed in the ribbons and feathers adorning the selection of bonnets in the milliners. She was halfway to a hundred when a familiar, loathsome voice hissed in her ear. "Do not turn around, just listen and mark my words well. Part of me wants very much to kill you now and see your blood spread across the cobbles, but the greater reward will be when I watch you as I kill the king and then of course, I shall take the greatest of pleasure in ridding the world of you and your damnable paramour. Here is a little reminder, a souvenir if you will so that you do not forget who you are dealing with." She felt a sharp sting underneath her ear. "History will show me to be a great man, the man who restored the glory of Britain after its decline since the days of the Tudors. You may be under the illusion that you have somehow foiled my plans, but I shall arise like a phoenix from the ashes. I need no-one, I am invincible." And as soon as he had appeared, he vanished into the milling market day crowd.

CHAPTER 34

"I cannot believe how close you came to danger with that blackguard," Stephen said, enfolding her in his arms as they lay on the bed. "He must have been watching us and when I left you, saw his moment to pounce. He could have killed you."

"He is quite mad," she replied. "He could indeed have killed me but did not. Apparently, I or he is to have that pleasure later."

"My heart almost stopped when I saw you sitting outside the milliner's with blood down the front of your dress." His fingers delicately touched the fine white bandage on her neck.

"There is always a lot of blood with a flesh wound," she assured him.

"Yet an inch to the right and you would have bled to death, I know it, you know it, and I am damned sure Reece knows it," Stephen said, his voice tight with fury.

"I imagine he thought the better of cutting someone's throat in the middle of market day," she replied wryly. "Not good for business and not good for a man who wants to remain in the shadows for the time being, so I am here to fight another day."

"The question is, what will he do next? He is a man who will not give up whatever the cost."

"I think he is planning something spectacular, something that will be reported in the newspapers, he thinks only of himself, and he wants immortality or at the very least a place in history," Ella replied, thoughtfully. "I think he means to try to assassinate the king."

"Of course," Stephen replied. "His original plan was thwarted but an assassination will mean he is forever remembered, and it may be that his actions do in fact provide the spark for the revolution after all," he said then paused, "and I believe he wants us to know what he is planning."

"So that we rush to try and save the king, we see the heinous act, and he manages to exact his revenge on us too?"

Stephen nodded. "There is no time to lose."

As they set off as dawn was breaking Ella said, "Do you think we shall be able to get there in time? If Reece is travelling by horse, he will no doubt be quicker than us."

Stephen shook his head. "Under normal circumstances he would, however, it is my belief that he will take less travelled roads so as not to be apprehended. He has probably surmised by now that I have sent mail riders both to my men and to Carlton House to increase the king's guards. With any luck we shall be in London before him."

"Let us hope so," she replied.

"Try to get some rest, my love," Stephen said, "we shall change horses every fifteen miles so that we arrive in town as speedily as possible, and when we arrive, we shall have much to do."

They stopped only to wash and change their travelling clothes before going straight to Carlton House, entering through a side gate rather than the main entrance in Pall Mall. The young man who greeted them led them through a series of corridors and staircases until they were shown into the Crimson Drawing Room where the unmistakable figure of the king greeted them.

"Come in, come in, Hart," he boomed.

"Your Majesty," they said in unison as Stephen bowed and Ella curtseyed.

"Now," the monarch said, resting his great bulk on one of the crimson damask chairs. "Sit and tell me of this rebellion you have quelled."

He listened intently as Stephen related the tale, from intercepting the code to the events at Bolton Castle, leaving nothing out and ensuring that Ella's part in the proceedings received fair attention. "In fact," he finished, "were it not for Lady Ella's skill in deciphering the code and her bravery in the field of action, I believe we should not have been able to discover the details of the plot nor apprehend the plotters."

The king turned his attention to Ella, his eyebrows raised, "A woman in a man's world? We know there are those who believe that a woman is as capable as a man, though they are generally regarded as cranks."

"Perhaps one day, Your Majesty, women may be able to prove their worth in the world of Science and Mathematics as well as in the domestic sphere," Ella said.

"Then we men must be on our guard Hart, dangerous world if women take over, eh?" He chuckled.

"Indeed Sir," Stephen replied, "though there is still a clear and present danger whilst the man Reece is at large and we believe he will try to harm your person."

"Then what do you suggest?"

Stephen took a breath. "I believe we must draw him out."

The king looked at him steadily. "By that we assume you mean to place ourself in a position where this man may attempt regicide?"

"Sir," Ella replied, "would it not be better to lance the boil as it were, rather than live continually with the threat of Reece hanging over every public appearance or even insinuating himself in your household to do you harm?"

The king nodded thoughtfully. "Very well, what do you suggest?"

Ella was surprised to realise that her monarch was looking to her rather than Stephen. "I think Reece knows it is only a matter of time before he is caught so I think he will take the first opportunity for attack and I think also he will probably want it to be at a public event so that it is reported in the papers, he seems to crave attention and does not care whether it is for good or ill. Do you perhaps have plans to attend the theatre or give a ball or some such in the next few weeks?" she asked.

"There are no plans for any engagements here," he gestured to the lavish crimson and gilt room, "this is all to be packed and removed to Buckingham House, the improvements there are almost complete. However, a trip to the theatre can always be arranged, I believe there is a revival of The Rivals at Drury Lane, I shall attend there, a comedy is always welcome. We shall command that our box be made ready shall we say for in a week's time?"

Stephen nodded. "I had thought a ball here might be the thing, but on reflection, the theatre will be better. There should be fewer people and with limited entrances it should be easier to have someone to oversee them."

The king rose. "Very well. We shall leave the details to you."

"I have an idea," Ella said as she, Stephen and some of his trusted men sat around the huge mahogany table in his town house. "You have guards on the doors and in the audience as well as serving refreshments in the interval, but there is no-one on the stage. I think it would be a good idea for me to mingle with the players. I have seen the production before and there is a duel scene. What better opportunity for an assassin to point his weapon at the royal box when everyone's attention is on the stage?"

"A lady? On the stage? Think of the scandal. You would be ruined," one of Stephen's older men blustered.

"I should think the king being assassinated would be a greater scandal," Ella replied, drily. "In any case," she went on, "I should be disguised, perhaps as a page to Sir Lucas O'Trigger or Captain Jack Absolute."

"Who the devil are they?" The older man's eyes nearly popped out of his head.

She just stopped herself from rolling her eyes. "They are the duellers in the play, Sir."

Stephen pursed his lips. "Reluctant as I am to place her in further danger, I believe Lady Ella's idea is a sound one. She will be in costume and with her face painted I have no doubt she can pull off the role and will perhaps be easier to disguise than our fellows."

"I'll be 'elen Woods an orphan from 'ackney, tryin' to make me livin' as an actress guv'nor," Ella said, with an outrageous wink at the old man.

"Some of those actor fellows are not at all the thing," he was still unconvinced. "What about the lady's honour? As we know actresses are little more than..." He hesitated.

"For one thing, my lord," Ella replied, irritated that his comment was addressed to Stephen and not to herself, "no-one will be in the slightest bit interested in the lowest member of the company and for another, I believe I am more than able to protect myself from the unwanted attentions of any man, actor or gentleman."

Stephen nodded with a wry smile. "I can certainly testify to that."

In the four days before the king was to attend the performance, plans were carefully put in place. Strings were pulled so that Ella could become a member of the company and even attended rehearsals so that she would know the best place to stand in order to observe the other actors on the stage. A costume had been made for her to stand as a page to Captain Jack, an actor who was much admired by the ladies of the ton but whom, as Ella found when up close, was a lot older and, she suspected, wore a corset and Waterloo teeth. Without his wig and make-up, he would be passed on the street without a second glance. She was amused by her own costume of green satin breeches, silver waistcoat and green jacket with pockets to conceal the pistols and knives she would be carrying. The ensemble was finished with a dark wig and a small tricorn hat.

The morning of the performance, Stephen woke her and made love to her with an intensity neither of them had experienced before. "I cannot believe I have once again allowed you to put yourself in danger," he whispered into her hair. "Ella, you must know that you are the love of my life, the heart of my heart, the soul of my soul. Without you I am nothing but a shell of a man. When this is over, would you do me the honour of becoming my...."

"Shh," she said, placing a finger over his lips. "One day, our children may ask how and where you proposed, I do not think whilst we were in bed after making love is quite the answer we shall want to give," she said, giggling.

"Oh, my love," he said tenderly, "does that mean you will accept?"

"I cannot say duke, for I have not yet been asked," she replied, primly but with a wicked glint in her eye.

"Witch," he laughed, and made love to her again.

CHAPTER 35

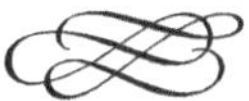

"I've had enough of this." Ella's ears pricked up as she overheard the leading actress speaking to her dresser from behind the screen where she was changing. "I caught that new stagehand creeping around the dressing rooms and putting paint on his face. I don't like it and I don't like him, after tonight's performance I shall tell the manager, either he goes or I go. In any case I've been offered the role of Lucy Locket in The Beggar's Opera at The Haymarket. Of course, with the king coming tonight the manager can't think of anything else, now lace me tighter, who knows what gentlemen will be coming backstage tonight."

Ella placed the bouquet the king had sent, on the dressing table among the pots of rouge, ash, white paints and enamels. The new stagehand had to be Reece, but there was little time to alert Stephen, in any case, she did not know where in the theatre he might be. She was already dressed for her part and made her way to the side of the stage where she could observe the stagehands setting the scenery with ropes, pulleys and weights, and suddenly, there he was, up high on the platform, tying the painted cloth to the frame. She stepped back, she could have shot him where he stood, but until he made an attempt on the king, she would have been guilty of killing a so-called innocent man. She would have to wait.

As the duelling scene approached, Ella's senses were heightened, she held the duelling pistols in the box as her part demanded, looking into the sides of the stage she could see several stagehands but none of them was Reece. In front of her, the two antagonists circled each other, neither, as the script demanded, was particularly keen to fight, as they approached to select their weapon; she was aware of another actor quietly entering the stage, she knew at once it was Reece. As the duellers took their ten paces, she saw his hand go towards a pocket in his costume. Of course, that was his plan, when the duelling pistols discharged enough powder to make a noise but with no shot, he would shoot the king, no-one would know where the shot had come from and in the ensuing panic if anyone did notice, he would slip quietly away.

As the duellers turned, she quickly took the pistol from her pocket and at the moment the shots were fired, she shot Reece in the knee, causing him to drop the pistol and fall to the floor with a cry. There was a shocked silence from the actors. "Well, Sirs," she said, making sure her voice was loud enough to carry to the audience, "I don't know which of you engaged this quack doctor who managed to shoot himself in the foot and faints at the sight of his own blood. I'll take him away Sirs and find a sawbones who can patch up whichever one of you wins and who'll cart away the loser." With that, she took the still groaning Reece by the boots and dragged him off the stage, to unexpected applause and laughter.

By the time she had dragged Reece backstage, the actors had continued with the play and Stephen appeared with four burly men who took Reece none too gently to a waiting closed carriage which would bear him off to Newgate prison. Regardless of their small audience of interested actors and stagehands, Stephen took her in his arms in a tight embrace. "It is over, thank God. Why did you not get a message to me?"

"We were already on the stage when he appeared, apparently he got himself engaged as a stagehand because one of the men did not appear for work earlier in the week."

"A man whom I suspect will probably be dragged from the Thames eventually," Stephen said, grimly.

"Quite possibly," she agreed.

"Why did you not take the lethal shot?"

"I had a chance earlier, but I wanted him to face judgement, otherwise I would have been no better than him in killing someone in cold blood. I could not live with myself had I done that," she replied, simply.

He dropped his head and rested it on her forehead. "You are truly a remarkable woman, beautiful, just, courageous and ..."

"Lethal?" she suggested.

"I was going to say, the only woman I have ever, or will ever love. Now come, let us go home."

Three nights later, Stephen bounded into the green drawing room where Ella was quietly enjoying the delights of Miss Austen's Persuasion. He had been mysteriously absent all day.

"Come," he said, holding out his hand. "There is something I want you to see."

They went into the garden where small lamps guided them towards the summer house which appeared to be lit by a hundred candles. As Ella entered the room her senses were almost overwhelmed by the scent of roses from the thousands of rose petals scattered on the floor. When they got to the centre of the room, Stephen went down on one knee. "This, I think, is the story we shall tell our children," he said. "Lady Ella Grainger, I have loved you almost since I first met you. I have never loved another woman and never will, there is only one woman in the world for me, and that woman is standing before me. Would you please put me out of my misery and consent to become my wife. I promise that I shall never put restrictions on you, and should we be blessed with daughters, I shall ensure that they have the best education and encouragement to live fulfilled lives whatever they choose to do."

"Of course I will marry you, I thought you would never ask," she teased, "and I love you too." Ella laughed and went willingly into his arms for a devastating kiss.

"I have a special licence," he said, patting his pocket. "If you are agreeable, we can be married as soon as tomorrow, though if you would prefer a larger affair, I am prepared to wait for a month, but that is all."

In the event, their wedding was grander than they had anticipated, the king, being grateful to his two loyal subjects, insisted that they marry in the Chapel Royal at St. James' Palace. Instead of the quiet ceremony they had anticipated, there were as many members of the ton present who could fit into the oak pews. As the fanfare sounded and Ella began her walk down the aisle, Stephen turned and the sight of Ella took his breath away. She was dressed in an ivory gown with a tulle overskirt that was embroidered with silver thread and diamante that shimmered as she walked. Her bridal veil was the finest Brussels lace and held in place by a coronet of white rosebuds which matched the bouquet she carried. He could not take his eyes off her, nor could he remove the grin from his face as she approached. Finally, in a few short minutes, she would be his and his alone.

Ella gave him a shy smile as turned and handed her bouquet to Verity, her matron of honour. As the minister began the age-old words, Ella felt encircled by a cloak of love, Stephen would love and cherish her as her father never had as she would love and cherish him for the rest of her days.

After the ceremony, they made their bow and curtsey to the

king, who wiped a tear from his eye with a large, snowy white handkerchief. "Good luck getting this one to obey you," he said to Stephen, slapping him on the back. "Congratulations to you both, may I kiss the bride?"

Stephen nodded, he was the king after all.

Two days later, a summons arrived for the newlyweds to attend His Majesty at Carlton House. "I was rather hoping," Stephen said, nuzzling Ella's ear because he knew it drove her wild, "that His Majesty would have remembered that we are newlyweds and have other matters on our minds." His hand drifted towards her breasts and teased an already hardening nipple.

"I do not believe his own experience of marriage is considered positive, ahhh," she gasped.

"Would you like me to stop, Duchess?" He quirked an eyebrow and could not help teasing her.

"Good God no," she murmured, as his hand drifted lower.

"I suppose we must attend. Though while I am speaking with His Majesty, bear in mind, this is what I am thinking of." She was under him and her legs parted to receive him as his cock sought her entrance. They moved together until they were slick with sweat and satiated for the third time that morning. "Also bear in mind that there are twenty rooms in this house and I intend to have you in all of them," he said.

"You are quite insatiable," she sighed.

"You make me so," he replied. "And though I want to lock the door against the world, we had better bathe, dress and obey the king's command."

"Ah, the newlyweds," the king boomed as soon as they had made their bow and curtsey. "And I must say you are both looking very satisfied," he smirked. "I understand that you are to take a honeymoon journey shortly."

"Yes, Your Majesty, we are to visit Paris, Vienna, Venice and Rome among other places," Stephen explained. "My wife has a yearning for travel, and I thought we should go before the next war breaks out. As it surely will."

"As to that point, there may be something you might do for your country whilst you are there," the king said.

"I am sorry, Sir, but my days as an agent are over," Stephen said, firmly. "But should serious need arise, Sir, you have my word I shall be at your service." He looked at Ella. "As shall my wife."

"A woman in the service, intriguing and quite right too, you have won your spurs my dear as the saying goes. And further to that, we have been thinking of a suitable reward for services already rendered. Duke, you shall of course be presented with a medal with our grateful thanks, though as you know it cannot be worn other than in the company of those who know what it is."

He turned to Ella. "There is no precedent for a woman to be awarded a medal so we have devised a reward we believe is appropriate. Your father's title is now defunct as no living male heirs could be found, we know that land and the house were sold to your brother-in-law, but the title reverted to the Crown. It is with great pleasure that we bestow on you the title of Countess of Swallowfield and an income of five thousand pounds a year which shall pass to your firstborn daughter and progress down the female line and always be in the possession of a female whether she marry or no. You are a lady by birth, a duchess by marriage and a countess in your own right."

Ella sank into a deep curtsey. "You do me a great honour, Your Majesty."

He held out a hand. "No my dear, you did us a great service which we shall not forget. We men believe ourselves to be the masters of the universe because by and large, we rely on our superior strength to subjugate and subdue. You have shown me,

Countess, that women have fine minds and skills which we should be foolish to ignore. We cannot say that things will change overnight, but one day it shall come to pass that women are valued for their true worth."

"Perhaps," Ella said, with a twinkle in her eye, "one day, women shall rule."

"Well, let us not go that far." The king laughed and stood to indicate that the audience was over.

EPILOGUE

As the ducal carriage rolled down the long driveway, Ella could see the whole family standing on the steps to greet them, the younger children waving like mad, eager to meet their new cousin who slept soundly in her bassinet, well wrapped in the blanket against the cold, frosty December air. Her nursemaid, Ella's maid and Stephen's valet followed in the second coach with a third loaded with their luggage, but Stephen had refused to let his daughter out of his sight. He had even fashioned straps so that the bassinet would not be jolted on the icy ruts, although the turnpikes were slightly smoother, the journey from Wensley had been long and tedious and the travellers were all looking forward to spending Christmas at Swallowfield.

Elliott strode through the path cleared through the snow and opened the carriage door almost as soon as it drew to a halt. "Welcome, welcome," he said, "come in quickly and warm yourselves. The children are beyond themselves with excitement."

Stephen leapt down and reached back to retrieve his daughter, still sleeping peacefully in her bassinet, completely oblivious to the excited cries of children and barking of Elliott's Irish wolfhounds.

Ella stepped down and was quickly enveloped in a hug from her sister, Verity. "My goodness," Verity exclaimed, "your nose is like a little icicle, come inside before it drops off."

"I doubt that will happen," Ella laughed, but it is good to be here." At one time she would have said home, for Swallowfield was their childhood home, but home was now where Stephen was, their townhouse in London, the estate in Herefordshire, even the hunting estate in Scotland, but her favourite would always be Wensley.

As always, It delighted Ella to see Swallowfield restored to the glory it was before her father ran it down. Paintings had been restored and there was new furniture, carpets and drapes. There was a smell of beeswax as floors and furniture shone and the new chandeliers sparkled. There was the fresh smell of evergreens as the house had been decorated for Christmas with holly and ivy boughs on many surfaces and in the hall a magnificent tree decorated with candles and sweetmeats, a tradition Elliott had seen when travelling in Europe as a young man. Later, she would place the gaily wrapped gifts beneath it and could not wait to see the excitement on the children's faces as they opened their gifts. Even her daughter, Francesca, would have a silver rattle to play with, though she would of course have no memory of her first Christmas.

Later, as the adults sat in the rose drawing room, the men enjoying a game of chess with their port and Ella and Verity sitting by the fire quietly chatting, the children all in bed in the nursery. Stephen stole a glance at the wife he adored, her delicate profile lit by the oil lamp behind her. "We are, without doubt the luckiest men alive," he said to his brother.

"You will get no argument from me on that score," his brother agreed, looking at his own wife with love in his eyes. "And yours is now Countess of Swallowfield I believe, since the king decided to restore their father's title to her as the eldest offspring, and to be inherited down the female line. I do not believe I have heard the like before, rather a forward thinking move from His Majesty," he said, raising his eyebrows.

"Ella, like Verity, can be persuasive," Stephen commented, "as well as having many talents she has kept hidden."

"Like her talent for mathematics and deciphering?" Elliott asked. "Come, brother, I know you and she have been involved in some imbroglio. And the fact that the king was involved in the wedding caused something of a twitter within the ton. What can you tell me?"

"On the strict understanding that this remains purely between us, for that part of our life is now over. I have retired as an agent and could not be happier. I intend to devote my life to my family and my estates." Stephen replied.

"Of course, I know the value of secrecy."

"In any case, Ella's book of puzzles, codes and enigmas has been such a success, she could hardly engage in secret activities."

Stephen outlined the plot and how it and the assassination attempt had been foiled.

"My God," Elliott whistled. "It would seem our Ella has more hidden depths than I imagined."

Stephen glanced over at his wife with pride. "She certainly does, but I have discovered the secret of Ella's enigma."

Elliott looked at his brother questioningly.

"Love," Stephen replied. "It is really that simple, I may be a duke with power and influence, but at the end of the day, I am nothing, have nothing without Ella's love."

He glanced once more at his wife and caught her eye; the love he saw there took his breath away. "Love," he said, "is the greatest gift we have to give."

Elliott looked at his wife. "Amen to that brother, Amen to that."

ACKNOWLEDGMENTS

To everyone at Melange huge thanks for publishing my books and helping to make me a better writer by your tireless attention to detail and encouragement.

THANK YOU FOR READING

Did you enjoy this book?

We invite you to leave a review at your favorite book site, such as Goodreads, Amazon, Barnes & Noble, etc.

DID YOU KNOW THAT LEAVING A REVIEW...

- Helps other readers find books they may enjoy.
- Gives you a chance to let your voice be heard.
- Gives authors recognition for their hard work.
- Doesn't have to be long. A sentence or two about why you liked the book will do.

ABOUT THE AUTHOR

Anna lives in a pretty village in Hampshire, not far from the home of her literary heroine, Jane Austen, though she frequently enjoys spending time in the beautiful Yorkshire Dales, walking or just enjoying their majestic beauty. She has always enjoyed history and loves to visit stately homes to have a glimpse into the past where she imagines her heroes and heroines lived and loved.

When not writing, Anna runs a creative writing group and a playreading group as well as playing the piano and accordion, both badly. She would like to say she has the accomplishments demanded of a lady in the past, but sadly it isn't so, she started a piece of embroidery ten years ago and it's still not finished and her watercolours resemble a drunken fight between two spiders. Anna would, however, fit in with the Georgian ladies' habit of drinking copious cups of tea!

Anna's books always reference Christmas at some point because she loves celebrating with her family and friends, coming from a long line of women who loved making Christmas a memorable and magical time.

ALSO BY ANNA AYSGARTH

Unsuitable Brides

A Bride for Christmas

The Marquess Meets Miss Nobody

Never a Lady

To Marry a Duke

Ella's Enigma

Novels

The Making of Her

www.ingramcontent.com/pod-product-compliance
Lightning Source LLC
LaVergne TN
LVHW090600110826
845146LV00001B/201

* 9 7 9 8 8 8 6 5 3 4 5 5 9 *